MAGA HAT ROMANCE BOOK 1

LADIES FIRST

LIBERTY ADAMS

Published by Germane Press, LLC

ISBN: 978-1-7356830-1-0 (Paperback)
ISBN: 978-1-7356830-0-3 (E-book)

Cover Design by 100Covers.com
Interior Design by FormattedBooks.com

DEDICATION

This series is dedicated to MAGA Patriots everywhere.

ACKNOWLEDGEMENTS

For friends, family, fellow writers,
critics and coaches who helped me.
Thank you. And for President Trump,
whose MAGA movement inspired this series.

CONTENTS

Dedication III

Acknowledgements V

Chapter One I

Chapter Two 5

Chapter Three 15

Chapter Four 21

Chapter Five 29

Chapter Six 35

Chapter Seven 39

Chapter Eight 43

Chapter Nine 49

Chapter Ten 53

Chapter Eleven 59

Chapter Twelve 61

Chapter Thirteen 69

Chapter Fourteen 75

Chapter Fifteen 83

Chapter Sixteen 87

Chapter Seventeen 89

Chapter Eighteen 97

Author Bio 103

A Note To Readers 105

CHAPTER ONE

A red blur greeted Ricki from inside the rapid transit trolley car as it whizzed past and came to a stop. She adjusted the waistband of her low-slung jeans and took her place at the front of the throng waiting on the platform. Inside the car, not many were preparing to exit. She hated it when large events crowded the ridership on her line. This one, a Trump victory rally coming just weeks after President Trump's inauguration, explained all the red, making her hate it even more.

She braced herself for the inevitable pushing and shoving, even though the thought of getting anywhere near one red-clad rallygoer, let alone be surrounded by them—

The doors opened. She leaped forward, determined to make this car. Her destination was the same rally as many of the passengers she loathed. She had to get on now, before she lost her nerve and changed her mind about attending.

Riders spilled out, thwarting Ricki's progress. Room in the car was disappearing. And then, an opening.

From experience riding the line, Ricki knew just how to time her next move. She hunched down small, ready to shoot the gap. But a hulk at her left elbow stepped into it.

"Nooooo!" She grabbed the hulk's arm and tried to squeeze past.

The hulk stopped, then smiled when he saw her. Immediately, he stepped out of the way, blocking a wall of bodies. He ushered her forward with a gallant gesture.

"Ladies first," he said.

Ah, a redneck. The kind that drew her automatic disdain. Ricki scowled. For good measure, she used the toe of one of his steel-capped work boots as a stepping-stone and set her elbow in the vicinity of the hulk's ribcage. Men like this only existed in the world of her father and brother, who were holdouts to a version of masculinity that was rapidly disappearing. According to fourth-wave feminism, most of the rest should have been reduced to blithering apologetics by now.

Still, it was handy to have her way cleared. She stepped inside and searched for a strap or grab-room on the overhead bar. But the hulk hadn't finished.

"I insist."

A single empty seat remained. He continued to block the swell of commuters while he pointed at the seat, smiling at her to take it. Behind them, she felt many sets of eyes, all trained on that seat. What was he trying to do? This type she could dispatch with ease.

"You're holding up the show," she said. She grabbed hand space on the bar and glared at him.

"Oh, you do talk." He was still smiling.

She looked away, not knowing how to respond. In that second, Harold slithered between them and parked his butt on the empty seat. Harold was a regular on the line, like Ricki. Normally, she did her best to ignore him, but today she gave him a fist bump.

"Atta boy, Harold," she said.

The rest of the car laughed as the train moved.

"Loser!" came a voice. It wasn't clear who the shouter was targeting.

Harold sat with his knees closed, the very image of detoxed masculinity. He wore a black watch cap. A scrawny beard feathered his jaw. Ricki thought he was simply repulsive. He'd struck up a conversation with her, once, quietly suggesting they meet for coffee sometime, a topic she'd firmly quashed. She'd spent her entire graduate program perfecting the art of rejecting men. In this, her final semester, she could, and sometimes did, give lessons in it. She hadn't sat through a single miserable date in ages. In fact, she hadn't had a good date, either, but that wasn't the point. As a feminist about to graduate with a master's degree in gender studies, dating was a mark of shame. She'd had a few dates during her undergrad years, all of which began and ended in complete awkwardness.

Across the narrow center aisle, crowded with bodies, the hulk rumbled his disapproval.

"Huh-uh," he said. "You defile the memory of my grandfather." So, he was upset she didn't fall for his guy-games. She was about to cut him down to size verbally, along with his grandfather, but the purpose for her rally-attending mission made her clamp her mouth shut. She might need this guy later. He'd already furnished her with some juicy man-hate; fodder for the blog post she planned to write for her blog, *Petra's Parlance*.

Unlike some of the other passengers, his wardrobe gave no indication of his destination. She didn't know where he was headed. He wore a white, button-down shirt, the kind with the embroidered pony, like her father wore. The shirt was tucked into a pair of work pants with no belt. His heavy work boots were hulking and oversized, like the rest of him. A dusty imprint remained on the toe where she had stepped.

She kept her attention on him, mostly because of the way she was facing. His reach up to the overhead bar was easy, relaxed. His head nearly touched it, and his elbow was bent at a comfortable angle. She stood a head shorter—she had to stretch all the way up to reach. He was trim and fit, despite his size, with workingman's hands, large and rough, and his face was handsome in a rugged, rather than pretty, way. She glanced at Harold and immediately saw the difference. Man vs. Boy.

The man wore his hair in a Kennedyesque, frat boy cut, a feature she loathed, even though it was the same style as her dad. Did he also hunt? She swept away the thought. Her father's passion, if known by the Sisterhood, might have her application for membership revoked. Ricki couldn't bear to risk rejection from the university's most prestigious feminist activist group. Her last task remaining before her entry into full membership was to attend this rally and write a blog post about it. Then, after Friday's membership tea would come her long-promised reward to herself—a tattoo she'd wanted since she was a kid.

The festive mood on the train lifted her earlier dour spirits. If nothing else, these red-clad cultists had enthusiasm on their side. For a fraction of a second, she even looked forward to the rally. Then she remembered who she was; and her reason for going snapped her back to the present, and her mission. When the trolley stopped, she was at the door, the first passenger to step off. She wanted to get a good seat.

CHAPTER TWO

In this venue of perfect fools, Ricki decided, she was the Wise Mother. But it was a low bar to meet. All around her sat the alt-right dupes, each one a replica of the next, and all engaged in an absurd dance of handshakes and backslaps. These people were the locus of injustice, beneath contempt. The Sisterhood must see this. She pulled out her camera phone and snapped away at the incoming crowd, capturing some T-shirt and spandex-clad women. They smiled and waved as they passed. Ricki smiled back. She laughed inwardly at their ignorance of her motives. She began to relax at how easy this was.

She chose a seat in the front row near a set of risers occupied by the media. They were a mass of cords and tripods with cameras, all manned by techs trying not to trip over the stylish, on-air personalities. She wondered what it would be like to have to cover someone so offensive and full of hate. From here, she had a clear, though distant, view of the podium, with good lines of sight to the floor activity amidst the alt-right masses.

"Is this seat saved?" She would at least feign politeness. The spot was in front of a gaggle of suburban-type women—all well-coiffed and manicured. Who'd elected a pussy-grabbing rapist for their leader, over the most well-qualified candidate who happened to be a woman. The woman next to the chosen seat patted it and smiled, glancing at Ricki's green-toned, platinum pixie.

"It's all yours, hon," she said.

"Thanks," said Ricki and sat down. Hon. When was the last time she'd been called hon? Sometime in high school, by the nurse, probably. She pulled out her phone and tapped in a few notes—Hon. Misogynist. Disrespect. Lack of awareness.

Ricki sat back in her cushioned seat, taking in the upbeat crowd. She actually marveled at how different the mood was here—an almost infantile cheer. It was such a contrast with her own side's crowds—always accompanied by shouting and rage that often spilled over into violence.

Rage. Rage and anger had become driving forces in life, expressed by her one cosmetic indulgence of black nail polish and lipstick. Oh, and the hair. Green, her choice today, all served the rage. It fueled her activism against a world in a state of perpetual injustice. But rage was not the face for today. Especially not with this bunch. Rage was as out of place here as her hair and makeup colors, but so far, the makeup and hair hadn't caused more than a glance.

A cheer sounded across the arena. Two younger men carried one elderly man down the stairs and to his seat. A standing ovation on both sides of the aisle accompanied them. Ricki turned to the trad wife next to her.

"What's going on?" She pointed. Her seatmate studied the situation.

"A veteran," she finally said. "They do it a lot. WWII, Korea, Viet Nam maybe. The president loves to introduce them at rallies." She turned her attention on Ricki. For the first time she took in her hair, then her face, then glanced to her black painted nails. "This your first rally?"

So, people attend these more than once. "Yes," she said.

Veterans. People she almost never thought about. Veterans were certainly not people she and the Sisterhood openly celebrated. In fact, more than a few of them showed an open contempt that shocked even Ricki. Veterans, and even the police, she'd been taught growing up, were among the best and bravest Americans, even though no members of her family had served. Her friends ridiculed the notion of putting your life on the line to protect the country, and she'd always gone along with that attitude. And even though Ricki did not quite share it, she would never openly challenge their belief.

The woman was perky and cute. Her nose wrinkled when she smiled. "Welcome! Glad you came. I hope you have fun here."

"Sure," said Ricki. "It's great." She wondered how she could ask the woman about Blacks, gays, intersectionality. Nothing in her persona, her dress, or her casual conversing gave Ricki any clue to her views on race or injustice. In fact, for the nearly full hour Ricki had been inside the venue, she hadn't had even a glimpse of what she came to see. She decided to take a walk around the place, go racist hunting. She turned to the lady.

"Excuse me." She stood up slightly and put her hoodie on the chair. "I'm going to walk a bit. Could you save my seat, please?"

The woman, a redhead, smiled and stuck out her hand. "Of course, what's your name?"

Ricki wondered if she was shaking hands with an actual racist. "I'm Ricki," she said.

"Nice to meet you, Ricki, I'm Marilyn." The woman patted the seat of Ricki's chair. "See you later."

A promenade that separated the lower from the upper seating levels ringed the arena. Ricki strolled it, watching. Up above, seats were filling in quickly. Below, on the floor, swarmed almost unbelievable numbers of security. Some were venue employees in orange T-shirts, manning each section of seats, directing rallygoers here and there. One group, all dressed in identical, khaki-colored polos with matching work pants and sturdy black boots, caught Ricki's attention.

Ricki made her way back to floor level to get a closer look. They were fascinating to watch. All were young and muscular, even the two women she saw, and all but one of the men had full sleeve tattoos of varying designs. The women's tattoos were less prominent, but still visible. Ricki looked closely at the designs. She hadn't quite decided yet on her own tattoo design.

She watched one woman in particular. Olive-complected, she had coal-black hair pulled into a tight knot, large eyes heavily lined in kohl, and sensual, full lips. She was tall and shapely, beautiful, and very tough looking. Ricki doubted she would have much trouble taking down ninety percent of the attendees in the place. There were far more men in the corps—they were mostly just muscle-bound. Ricki wondered how they could run or jump. Their biceps and shoulders stretched the shirt material nearly to the ripping point, and their thighs resembled tree trunks. The posture of both the men and the women was spine-stiff straight, and they walked with a confident swagger. They seemed not at all distracted by the booming music or phased by the raucous crowd, now engaged in making an endless "wave" loop circling the arena, with people laughing like hell. Indeed, the security detail were intent on each other, keeping each other in sight, greeting each other when they passed. They watched the crowd closely, weaving among the folks standing on the floor in front of the podium.

She decided to go back up to the entrance lobby and find the restrooms. Uncertain of where to go, and a bit disappointed she hadn't spotted any overt racism, she was shocked when she turned a corner and nearly collided with a group of college-aged youth, several of them persons of color. Just as shocking were the whites in their midst. At least two of the group wore red MAGA hats. They all carried rally signs. It shattered her expectations. She'd ignored the sprinkle of Hispanics, Asians, and Blacks in the crowd as she waited in line earlier, thinking them merely outliers—betrayers to the resistance cause. But this, up close and literally in her face, she could not deny. As she tried not to gape, they stepped around her, pleasantly, smiling like the rest of the racists. One of them flashed a thumbs-up sign, what she'd been told was the president's secret sign to the whitest of his base. It would have made sense, except it was one of the Black youths who flashed it. She walked on, and then saw a stand that said Resolve Gun Club and Rifle Range.

Ah, pay dirt. No guns in sight, though, just signs and literature. But how to approach them? She walked up to a nearby table with T-shirts for sale and pretended to inspect the merchandise. Eventually, there was only one man with a full beard standing behind the gun club table. He smiled and touched the brim of a black felt cowboy hat.

"Good day, little lady," he said. "Would you like to become a member?"

She shook her head. "No," she said, "but I have questions."

"Ask away!"

"I'd like to buy an assault rifle."

The man's eyes narrowed. "What's an assault rifle?" he said. He wasn't smiling.

Ricki did not know what to say. Was he joking? "Well," she began, "you know, an assault rifle."

He stared at her like she was crazy. "No," he said, "I don't know."

Then she saw a poster of one, right behind him. It was a black metal rifle, bold and wicked looking. The sight of it made her hate juices flow. "There." She pointed. "Like that."

The man turned around and looked. He began to laugh. "Oh, that's what you're talking about." He looked at her more closely. "That's an AR-15. The AR stands for ArmaLite Rifle. You want to buy one of those?"

She nodded slowly. "Yes."

"Well, first you have to pass a background check." Background check? She wished she hadn't started this.

"Honey," he said kindly, "have you ever taken a firearm safety course?"

"No."

"Have you ever shot a gun before?"

"Yes," she said. "I've hunted with my father and brother, but that was a long time ago."

"Okay." He seemed to regard her a bit more seriously. He handed her a business card. "I suggest you start with the safety course. We offer them at the range, for free, through the NRA." The club logo and contact info were on the card. "You can find out more here."

Ricki looked at the card, hiding her disappointment. She halfway hoped he would tell her how easy it would be to obtain the hated rifle; offer some kind of insider loophole information she could share with her Sisterhood friends and on the blog.

"Thanks," she said. She had a sudden idea. "Hey, can I get a picture with you?"

The man looked puzzled but shrugged. "Sure," he said.

Happy to have one small thing work out to her advantage, she recruited a passerby to snap a picture. The black rifle poster made the perfect backdrop, though it lacked the cachet of blatant racism. It would be proof of her attendance. Maybe she could find someone else to get a photo with.

"Thanks," she said. She walked away, then turned back to wave. He had his hands on his hips and was looking at her, with a slight air of suspicion.

No racists yet, but guns. She was getting close. She decided to go back to her seat, strike up a conversation with her seatmate. Perhaps her friends might spill the beans on their certain racism. All she needed was one. And then she stopped.

It was another man, walking toward her, with a Democrats for Trump T-shirt. A traitor! From her own party. But at least they could find some common ground in the party. It didn't seem she needed to have an excuse to talk to people. Everyone was exceedingly friendly, even kind. Feeling nearly desperate for some validation of her original theory that she would find the true hatred on this side of the divide, she approached him.

"Excuse me?" She stuck out her hand. "My name is Ricki."

The man shook her hand. Like every other person in the place, he had a warm, friendly manner, completely open and sincere.

"Hi, Ricki."

"I saw your T-shirt, and I was wondering, would you mind answering a few questions?"

"Are you a journalist?"

She wasn't. Not really. "No," she said, "I'm a graduate student, but I'm a Democrat, like you."

The man's smile grew bigger. "Welcome," he said. "Ask away."

In this hall full of people who were complete aliens to her, Ricki was not sure how to phrase her questions, or what to ask first. But, as a Democrat, he could, she hoped, clear up some misconceptions.

"So, you voted for this guy?"

The man looked down at his shirt. "Trump?" he said. "You betcha. He's taking care of the country, us, the little guy, like no other president, ever. So, yes, I voted for him. Good day, Miss."

Miss. Good day. What was with these men, anyway? She thought of the "ladies first" redneck in the trolley car. Were they all like this?

"Wait," she said.

He turned back. "Yes?"

"Aren't you afraid of being called racist?"

The man threw back his head and laughed. "If that's the worst thing I'm ever called, I'm doing pretty well."

What did he mean? "Yeah, but you're here, with these . . . people. You're one of them."

"One of what . . . racists? I'll get a tax break with more take-home pay; add to my kids' college fund. Because of him I can quit my extra job. We are planning for my wife to quit her job and stay home to raise the kids. We've talked about homeschooling.

So for us, the numbers are way, way better, know what I mean? If that makes me a racist, well, so be it."

Numbers may not lie, but she hated listening to this guy. He was spouting the talking points so ridiculed by the media. She had nothing but contempt for these people for voting with their pocketbooks. She steeled herself for what she knew was coming.

"I've lost friends over supporting this president, but, like I said, my family is doing way better, and I can see a bright future for my kids."

Beneath her skin, Ricki felt a flush of anger. In front of her stood a major traitor to her party, his party, the resistance, their movement, the very country itself. This man was standing up for a proven racist, by his own admission, by not denying it. By cavorting at this rally, and happily, with people who had voted for one.

He pointed toward the arena. "Those people want to raise their families and be left alone. They're not going to hurt anyone." He touched the word Democrat on his shirt. "It's these people. These people who are hurting the country. So, Miss." He touched the brim of his MAGA cap. "Now you know why I'm at the rally. I hope I've answered your question. Have a good day."

He walked away, leaving her shocked by his speech. What he had told her was the truth as he saw it, but to Ricki it was double-speak meant to cover up the intolerance of the marginalized. She leaned against a wall and looked hard at the people rushing past her, all smiling and laughing, getting seats, crowding around the souvenir table. It was a display of diversity she seldom saw any-where. More men were at the gun club table. Several young men were engaged in conversation. Smiles, laughter, arms waving and big gestures—the sort of things she despised about men. More worrisome was the lack of material for the blog post she had to write. She had encountered almost nothing of stereotypes and would be forced to embellish the gun guy and the suburban housewife seatmates. The rest would have to be conjured up.

She took out her phone to take shots with her camera. While she thought she wanted to get random and candid photographs of the people here, for her blog post, it was difficult to stay true to the stereotype attendee. Women, of all colors, sizes, and economic levels, were everywhere. In fact, there must be at least as many women, if not more, than men. She captured on screen a group of typical white guys, four in number walking together. They wore matching T-shirts. Upon closer inspection, she was disappointed to read Firefighters for Trump. Could she make something out of white male firefighters? Better than nothing. She snapped a pic, with little enthusiasm. But her biggest problem, she realized, was eliminating young people, Asian, Hispanic, and Blacks. Nearly every frame contained minorities—the marginalized. She managed to click off a few totally white frames, but not nearly as many as she had expected. When she heard a huge roar from the crowd, she hurried back to her seat. It was her last chance, she thought, to find proof in the pudding. And that pudding would be Donald Trump. Surely, there would be plenty of angry propaganda when he came out on stage. Ricki had a good ear for the alt-right's dog whistles. She would listen carefully to every word the president said.

CHAPTER THREE

I f the Republicans didn't use the word God so much, thought Ricki, they might be worth listening to. To help pass the time, and also to gather material for a clever lead-in to her blog post, Ricki decided to count the number of times the president used the name God in his speech. Even with the warm-up speakers— politicians, campaign personnel, and other public figures—God was freely invoked. If she also counted the Pledge of Allegiance, and the two black women now leading the crowd in prayer, Ricki might have run out of fingers for counting before the president even took the stage. She wondered how the Star-Spangled Banner escaped without the mention of His name. In her own activist experience, Ricki could not recall anyone on her side using God as Supreme Being, guiding force, or higher power, although she had heard the name taken in vain. Many times.

Ricki bowed her head for the prayer and stared at the tips of her toes. She could not help but peer up at the two black women onstage. The sight was even more unsettling than the diverse crowd of attendees she'd encountered earlier. If Trump was a racist, if his supporters were racist, then why were these ladies given such a respected role? Even more puzzling was the lack of reaction of the people in the audience. Nobody, except her, seemed to think this was anything unusual at all. She glanced sideways at Marilyn to find her prayerfully engaged. Her eyes were shut, her hands folded. Her lips were moving slightly, her head nodding.

Ricki was discreet enough to wait to address Marilyn until they finished praying. "Who are those women?" she asked.

"Diamond and Silk," she said, without taking her eyes from the two retreating figures. As the raucous applause died down, Marilyn finally looked over at Ricki and grinned. "Two sisters from North Carolina. They're famous supporters, since 2015. Aren't they great? Everyone loves them."

Ricki didn't know exactly what Marilyn meant by 2015. Perhaps it referred to the early campaign. But a bigger mystery was the prominence of these two women of color, before what was supposed to be a racist crowd. Along with other jarring sights at this rally, it didn't match up with her definition of racism. But if she had to define racism, Ricki was not certain that what she saw here would fit. She pushed the thought away. That was impossible. The idea that these folks did *not* hate people of color or were *not* homophobic, that they accepted diversity, simply conflicted too strongly with her worldview. Hers was the anti-racist and tolerant bunch. The people she sat with now were the haters. Not only did they hate whoever did not look like them, they were uncouth and uneducated. Marilyn, for instance. Marilyn's zeal for anything and everything happening at this rally was getting on her nerves. Didn't the woman have any self-awareness? Did she realize how she was broadcasting her bigotry with her constant arm-waving and fist-pumping? And she didn't even apologize for all the times she bumped Ricki's shoulder when she jumped up from her seat.

Ricki sat back and sulked. She considered leaving the venue, except that she was on a mission. There must be another explanation for what she had been witnessing. Something simple that explained away the contradiction. Of course there was, but that was not her concern at the moment. Her purpose today was to blog about the rally, increase her readership for *Petra's Parlance*, and fulfill her final requirement for Sisterhood membership. Membership far outweighed in importance these assaults on her senses, these seeming anomalies. She must be willing to sacrifice for the sake of her side. There was nothing to do but wait for the main event.

It came quickly, almost unexpectedly. When "Proud to be an American" boomed through the speaker system, the crowd went to its feet. The roar as the president walked onstage was overwhelming. She sighed with relief. In an hour or a little more, this circus would come to an end. In the meantime, she would pay attention to the man who was, perhaps, the person she most loathed in all the world. She brought up the Notes app on her phone. She wanted to get some good quotes.

It took some time for everyone to quiet down. He began with remarks on the size of the crowd before moving quickly to bash the media. That Trump and the press had a hostile relationship was something that Ricki knew well. Every night on the news the press fought valiantly against the president's attempts to suppress reporters from informing the public of his malfeasance and corruption. It disgusted her that he actually used his contempt of the media to fire up the crowd.

"You see these people," he said, pointing his finger and sweeping his outstretched arm in front of him. "Back there. The fake news. If Pocahontas and Sleepy Joe ever had a crowd like this, the dishonest media would be turning their cameras every which way, letting the viewers see the audience. But with me, they keep the frame tight and square on me, so the viewers can't see that we have standing room only inside, with many times more watching outside on the Jumbotrons."

The crowd booed on cue. Ricki, unable to help herself, looked at the media risers. The camera operators did not take the bait. Their lenses remained frozen in place, trained directly on the podium. As the boos sounded through the arena, the president shook his head in disgust, then he stepped back from the mic and strolled the stage, taking in the crowd. Someone started a chant of "U-S-A."

He seemed totally at ease. In here, surrounded by his sycophant supporters, there was no failed administration and no chaos in the White House. The threat of imminent indictment simply did not exist. She'd been waiting a long time for his indictment. It seemed everybody was. But he did not appear at all to be a man about to be perp walked from the White House in handcuffs, locked up, with his fortune, his life, and his reputation in ruins. Indeed, he joked, smiled a lot, and even engaged in banter with the audience. The venue was filled with a rock concert-like atmosphere.

It was another thing Ricki saw but could not believe. This guy was a crook? He must be, she thought, after all the media and her friends told her this night after night. It was one of her and her roommate Karen's favorite topics of discussion. But here was the 2020 election in plain sight, with not even a whimper of a charge. But then, what did she expect? He was a billionaire. Therefore, untouchable. At least so far.

But there was one thing Ricki was forced to agree with. Even though many of her Sisterhood colleagues reviled the military, Ricki felt a wellspring opening up at the president's support of the veterans. For sure, it was a true crowd pleaser. Her applause for this one was genuine, whereas before, her reactions were carefully timed and calibrated.

Ricki checked her phone for the time. The president had been on stage for nearly an hour. She sat tight, still listening, although she was beginning to scan her notes and add to them. Her notes contained an arsenal of material from which she would tease out the coded language and stretch the truth just enough to spin into a damning blog post worthy of going viral.

Ricki congratulated herself when the president finished. She checked the time again. She was in no hurry, with the exits now clogged with rallygoers. She continued to type out notes, and made a call to Karen, her roommate, to tell her what time she expected to be home. She would try and make the 10:00 p.m. trolley.

CHAPTER FOUR

By the time the president boomed his last signature, crowd-roaring ". . . we will make America great again" chant, Mike had one man-sized crush on a pint-sized woman, just from watching her. Green hair, black lips. Easy to pick out, even when the crowd was on its feet, cheering, which was often. She'd sat mostly quiet, although a few times he caught her quietly applauding, occasionally standing, perhaps caught up in the mood of the ladies all around her.

But outside at night, in a river of people all trying to exit, her dark clothing and small size made her almost disappear. So, he watched her closely, fascinated by her, but alert to the threats posed by the protestors, anti-fascist especially. The police would be few and far between in the vast parking lot on the outskirts of the venue, and their assistance could not be counted on. Clearly out of her element, he needed to be her eyes and ears.

After the rally, she hunkered down in her chair, texting like mad, taking an occasional call. Mike did the same. Security shooed her out of the arena once the sea of attendees thinned. He made his exit, too, but stayed out of her field of vision. She was on the phone again. He could see her head tilt this way and that as she walked, her focus on her conversation. Perhaps she was paying only enough attention not to trip. As unaware as she was, she needed watching over and there was only one soul in this whole crowd who was willing to do it. He was his grandfather's boy and Mike knew very well how useful his type could be. He didn't take her hostility in the trolley car personally. All he wanted was a chance to talk to her.

Mike scanned their surroundings for threats, then focused in on her. For such a small body, she had a strong build. She had straight shoulders with a tiny waist cinched in with a narrow belt, her shirt tucked into a snug pair of jeans. Her breasts were firm and well-shaped. Nice to look at.

In the amber glow of the parking lot lights, he watched the pelting rain grow heavier. She had no coat, only a hoodie tied around her waist. This she untied and slipped into. She skirted the crowd, keeping her phone in her hand, her vision trained on the screen. That hoodie wasn't enough to keep a pissant warm, let alone dry, and with this rain, a serious chill would catch her before long.

Something slammed him, hard, from behind. He stopped, pissed off he'd let his attention wander. He knew what it was. Anti-fascists—the black-hooded figures and bandanaed faces gave them away. Somehow, they'd managed to infiltrate the throng of peaceful rallygoers without attracting attention. The punks ran and jumped through the crowd, tripping people, pushing and shoving, stirring up mayhem. He reached out to a couple of them and pulled down their masks. At least three set on him, but it was like taking out his sisters. Two quick shoves and a boot in some jerk's belly and he was free.

He looked at the girl-sprite. She was surrounded by them, paying attention now. They were pushing her, raising bike locks and bats at her, screaming and taunting, driving her backwards and further away from him. He saw her stumble, unable to escape the bullies. Why they'd chosen to pick on her he couldn't fathom. All he knew was they'd chosen wrong.

One of them shoved her. He saw her step backward into the punk's partner in crime; she raised her arms to try to shield herself. Her phone flew from her grasp. Now her attention was fully on the bullies. Self-preservation became her goal. A few men tried to intervene, but the anti-fascists soon overwhelmed them with their numbers. They beat back the men, two or three to one, who had to retreat to save their own skins.

Just as he reached her, something bumped his foot. Her phone. She saw it at the same moment. She dove for it, but one of the bullies caught her in the side with his boot and bent her double. She howled and went to her knees but managed to stand up again.

The bullies swarmed in and surrounded her. Mike stepped in, intending to make Jell-O out of the coward who kicked her in the ribs. His big body easily broke the wall of wimps, who turned on him. He swooped low, grabbed the phone, and shoved it in his coat pocket. On his way up he slammed into the pricks who'd assaulted her, then saw the one who'd put his shoe into her side. He plowed his elbow into the guy's nose; a crunch and a scream followed. He felt like Moses parting the Red Sea as he grabbed her wrist to pull her out of the melee. Escape time. She fought him, pulling back, thinking he was with the assault group.

"Let's go." He yanked harder than he wanted, but it was past time to flee. All around them was an unholy mass of black-clad punks, more than he could count, creating a ribbon of rage and violence. He steered the two of them, running, away from the crowd, pulling her after him. Even in this heightened state he was careful not to grip too hard and bruise her wrist. Christ, it was so small. She still resisted—he couldn't blame her for that. She had no idea who he was or where he was taking her, but she was no match for his strength, anyway.

"Let go!"

He stopped and took her by the shoulders. He could hear the mob behind them, interspersed with the rallygoers. It sounded like a full-blown riot. The throngs were making their way toward the exit gates, to their cars, to the trolley stop. He grabbed her tighter and shoved his face into hers.

"Come with me. There isn't time to explain." Her shoulders heaved from fright, from adrenaline, from the exertion, but she understood. He caught in her expression a glimpse of recognition of him as the man from the trolley. She nodded, her eyes wide.

"You'll get hurt," he said, "we'll get hurt. We've got to get out of here. These guys don't mess around. They want blood. Yours, mine, whoever. But yours is easier to take than mine."

"But . . . the cops—" She was on the verge of hysterics.

"Have a stand-down order." She probably hated cops. They all did, until a situation like this arose. But her fear shone like a beacon. She was terrified. Rightfully. At least she now had a sense of the danger. The crowd behind was losing its cohesive movement. The anti-fascists were creating small systems of chaotic reaction as pockets of rioting broke out. He softened his tone, certain now she was ready to listen to him. "Stay with me. And hang on to my hand."

"My phone!"

"I've got it. We're out of time. Now, let's go."

She nodded in agreement with small, quick up and down jerks of her head. Better. Now that she was with him, they would make faster progress. They took off again, running harder this time. He could feel her, still behind him, urging him forward, not pulling back anymore.

They reached the last row of cars and sprinted toward the exit gate. Some of the crowd hurried behind them. Mike threw a quick backward glance in the direction of the mob assault. The smell of smoke was accompanied by flames of orange on the black sky. Against the flames, against the light of the parking lot, the rain kept falling. He was glad he hadn't brought his truck here, even though he needed some way out of the danger.

"What's a stand-down order?" She shouted through her panting. He wondered why she was asking that now.

"It means don't do your job." Talking hurt his lungs, made him gasp for breath. "Don't ask questions. Just run."

They reached the gate. He pushed her through, in front of the cars that sat, bottlenecked, waiting for directions from traffic control. They exited onto the sidewalk of a side street. Mike steered them toward the nearest traffic light. They were alone now. It was quieter away from the crowd, and he hoped, the punks. They stopped to wait for the traffic light. He took his phone from his pocket. The time read 9:15 p.m. He dialed his foreman, Ronan Hassert.

"Ronan!" His breath was heavy.

"Boss." Ronan was his relaxed, casual self.

"Need some help here, Ro. Ran into some trouble. I need you to come and get us."

"Us?"

"I'll explain later. Just meet me on 35th. We're heading west. South of Greentree."

"Right."

Mike hung up.

"I'm not going with you anywhere."

He was getting pissed. "Just shut up and run."

He took her hand again, more firmly, and kept running. She was dragging behind, protesting the punishing pace. He slowed to a fast walk. Finally, he saw Ronan's truck turn onto the street just ahead of them and stop. Mike pulled open the door of the rear cab and turned to her, ready to hoist her inside.

"Oh, no." She set back on her heels. He didn't know how she had the strength to resist like this.

"Oh no, what?"

"I'm not going anywhere with you."

"Do you know what we just escaped from? They get paid to do this. They'll keep coming. All you are to them is something not bloody enough." She didn't move, only stood there in defiance of him. Mike shrugged and dropped her hand.

"Your choice." He didn't have time to argue. In the driver's seat, Ronan was turned around, watching them, halfway smiling. Mike climbed in and sat down, then looked down at her. "I'm not staying here. Get in now, or you're on your own."

He reached for the door handle.

"My phone!"

He tossed it to her. She caught it.

"I'll call you an Uber," he said. "Stay where you are."

He started to close the door.

"Wait."

"Well...?"

She stuck out her hand. "What's your name?"

Like it would help matters. Was she serious? "Mike. And we can't wait all night."

"Mike what?"

"Mike what? I can't even—Jorgensen, okay?"

The girl-sprite stuck out her hand. "Hi, Mike Jorgensen, I'm Ricki. Ricki Ellis."

From the front seat, Ronan began to laugh.

Mike shook hands. "Well, okay, Ricki Ellis. This is Ronan. Ronan, this is Ricki."

"Hello, Ricki."

"Hi, Ronan."

"Okay, can you get in now?"

He saw her hesitate, then glance toward the arena. The mob was still out there. She vaulted through the partially closed door like a scared rabbit, landing on top of him. For a moment, he held her in his lap, feeling her tremble. He slammed the door shut.

"Go, Ro."

Her dripping form tumbled over him into the opposite seat. She hugged the door, looking at him as if she might be his next murder victim.

Ronan hung a U-turn and turned back. As the streetlights washed through the truck's interior, he saw she was still trembling. Fright, cold. He took off his jacket.

"Up the heat, Ronan, would you? Thanks."

He scooted an inch toward her, holding up the coat. The inside would be warm from his body heat. Carefully, he draped it over her. His grandfather would be proud.

"Take this."

She shot him a look but snugged it in close to her. Her hair was matted flat to her head from the rain. The black makeup was smeared and running down her cheeks. Given her condition, it fit. Like she was orphaned or something. Like she needed love. He felt sympathy and protectiveness, even though she'd been an asshole earlier on the train.

"You gave me this because you think I'm weak."

"Well, at the moment, aren't you? If you don't like it, you can give it back."

"Hey, you two," said Ronan. "Boss, where to?"

Mike thought for a moment. He wanted to get his truck, now parked in his driveway. It was left home in favor of the trolley. But he was uncertain. He wanted a stiff drink, too. But he needed to eat, and he could use some strong coffee. He turned to Ricki.

"What was your name again? Sorry." He felt like a jerk for not remembering her name. After all, he'd just saved her from a vicious mob attack.

Her eyes shifted to see him. She was sullen in her little corner bunched up like a heap of laundry he might leave on the floor.

"Ricki."

He'd get her home safe and sound, but first . . .

"Yeah, Ricki. You hungry?"

She just sort of made herself smaller and didn't answer.

"Well, I want some coffee. You want coffee?"

This time she nodded. He could see the earrings in her ears as they bobbled up and down in the dimness.

"Drop us at the diner, would you, Ronan?"

"Sure, boss."

Ronan put his foot to the gas and sped on through the night.

CHAPTER FIVE

Two mugs clattered onto the counter. Hot, black coffee poured into his cup. Sally, the waitress working the counter tonight, eyed him. "Blonde and sweet?"

Mike looked at Ricki, then at Sally. "You said it, sailor."

They both laughed as she slid over the cream and sugar. They always shared this joke.

"Coffee?"

Ricki was staring at both of them like they spoke a foreign language. The girl needed to relax a bit if she ever hoped to get through a meal in this place. She looked down into her lap. Her lips moved. She mumbled something.

"What? Speak up." The waitress looked at Ricki with one brow arched. The pot of coffee was clutched in her fist, a bit like a hot poker she might use.

"Yes, please." Coffee splashed into the empty mug.

The waitress stalked off.

"Just what the hell did that mean?" she said. "Blonde and sweet?"

"Yeah, like women. Get it?"

Her mouth turned down in a pout.

"Here, let me show you." He tipped up the cream pitcher. "Blonde." His coffee changed from rich brownish black to caramel colored.

"Now, sweet." He dumped sugar into his spoon and stirred up his coffee. "You rad feminists need to learn to relax. It's a joke, okay? Got nothing to do with you."

Except . . . there was a head of striking blonde hair beneath the green shit. On second thought—

"Don't you ever get tired of that?"

"Tired of what?"

"Being mad all the time."

Her jaw clenched again. "I'm not mad."

He wanted to say more, but then she reached for the sugar and cream for herself.

"Ah, somebody who knows what good coffee's all about."

"I thought you believed in ladies first." She carefully poured out measures of cream and sugar and stirred them into her cup.

"Touché," he said. If he looked past the anger, he could see in her the barest hint of sweet.

Sally plopped down the order book. She scribbled without looking at Mike. "Your usual?"

"Yes, please."

This time she glanced up at Ricki.

"Just coffee."

"Why aren't you eating?"

The hands went to her lap again, twisting a ring on her finger. "I didn't bring any money."

"Hey, I'm the one who dragged you out of the rain and away from the mob against your will. I'm buying."

Her cheek and ear were turning pink. He ignored her embarrassment and turned to the waitress.

"Sally, bring her what you bring me. I'm not eating alone."

"Sure thing, Mike."

"Wait." She waved away the menu Sally held out. "Grilled cheese with fries, please. Whole wheat."

Sally wrote out the order then refilled their coffees.

Ricki sat back and looked around the place, seeming to like what she saw. She sipped. Her jaw unclenched. She even raised her cup. "Cheers."

Their eyes met as he lightly clinked his rim to hers. "To intersectionality."

"Are you making fun of me?"

"Of course not," he said, pretending to be offended. "Intersectionality works for everybody, if you think about it."

"No, it doesn't. You don't know what you're talking about."

"Of course, I do. You think you get to make the rules, but your rules only exist in your twisted world. It's not even a word. If you're intersectional for what, being female, with green hair and white—"

"I'm one-quarter Mexican."

"—then I'm intersectional for white and male, and Scottish-Swedish descent and that makes me less than human, at least according to your people, right?"

She scoffed. "You're so sure you know it all. It's just your white—"

"Male privilege." He sighed. "I still say it goes both ways. And my rule is just as legitimate as yours. In fact, more so. You've got one sliver of the universe who believes the way you do. I've got everything else on my side."

He expected back a dose of shrill female invective, railing about mansplaining but all she did was glare, like she couldn't think of anything to say. He stared back, thinking what pretty blue eyes she had. After a few seconds, she looked away. He wasn't going to budge an inch with this one. At another time in his life he would have let this type nail him. Not anymore. Michelle, his sister, had helped a lot with that.

Ricki's hands were small. They barely fit around the cup. A ring, petite like her, set with a green stone, circled her middle finger. He reached over and touched it, very lightly. The tip of his finger covered the stone.

"Nice.

"Thanks." She studied it. "It used to belong to my grandmother."

The repartee was interrupted by Sally's elbows as she plunked down plates. Hot sauce and ketchup followed. Mike screwed open the hot sauce bottle and turned to her.

"So, why'd you give away my seat earlier, on the subway?"

"I didn't give it away, you did."

"I saved it for you. I would've sat there myself."

She shrugged and sipped her coffee. "Wasn't your seat."

"Do you not like people being nice to you? You reject guys when they act like gentlemen?" He pointed to her ring. "You got that from your grandmother. Well, I had a grandfather who taught me to treat women with respect. Ladies first was always his motto. It's mine, too."

"Gentlemen?" She spoke the word with contempt. "They're useless."

"Useless? I saved your ass from a mob out for blood."

She paused. "Yeah, thanks."

"What were you doing at the rally?"

"Research for a blog post I'm writing."

"Oh, yeah? What blog?"

"It's called *Petra's Parlance*. Not that you've ever heard of it."

"Who's Petra?"

"Me."

"You're right, I never heard of it."

"That's because you probably just watch Fox News or read Breitbart."

"All of the above. Plus, Investor's Business Daily."

"Ah, yes," she said. "That conservative business rag? I might have known. Anyway, I'm hoping this post gets me some readers."

"Well, *Petra's Parlance*, I suppose you'll tell the world about all the redneck racists."

"That's the idea." She grinned and stuffed a fry into her mouth.

"So, I'll be the big bad racist spewing hate speech while a vicious redneck mob tried to attack you for wearing a Hillary T-shirt."

"Something like that."

"And how many did you find?"

"Several." She twirled another fry into her ketchup.

He chewed on his inside lip a bit, trying to figure something out. He drew out his phone from his back pocket and sat back in his chair. "No, how many did you actually talk to? Give me a number."

"You'll find out when you read it."

"What you mean is zero. So, you'll just lie about it."

Ricki, shrugged. "Doesn't matter," she said. "All that matters is balancing out the historic oppressors with the oppressed."

"Yeah, right, and what did you say the name of that blog was?"

"*Petra's Parlance.*"

He typed into his search bar. "Let's see here—'How to Incorporate Activism in Your Daily Life,' 'Radical Chic on a Budget.' And you're Petra?"

"That's right."

"Nice pen name."

"Thanks. I like it."

He scrolled through the phone, looking carefully at the screen. "God, this is some great reading, here. Thanks, Petra."

"More coffee?" Sally raised the pot in question, ready to pour.

"Sure," said Mike. "You're dangerous with that pot tonight."

"My weapon of choice."

"None for me, thanks," said Ricki. She turned to him. "Hey, it's been great. Thanks for all your help. And thanks for the meal. This is a great place. It really is. But, well, how can I get home?"

"I'll take you. I live with my twin sister, two blocks over. We'll walk there and get my truck."

He grabbed the check from the counter.

"Let's go."

CHAPTER SIX

If she were a different female, he'd be holding her hand. He'd wrap it, small and soft, in his larger, rougher one. She could be, would be, his girl. He shook his head to get rid of the image. It could never happen. Not possible.

Instead, he asked, "Where's home?"

"My parent's house. It's not too far from here."

"You still live with your parents?"

"No, I have an apartment with my best friend. But I'd rather stay at their house." She inched closer to him. "Do you always get riots at those rallies?"

"I don't know," he said. "Never went to a rally before."

"What did you think?"

He chuckled and grinned at her. "What do you think I thought?"

"You liked it?"

"Damn right I liked it. Awesome to be in company with such great patriots."

"Patriots. I haven't used that word since grade school."

"We are the greatest nation in the history of the world, you know. Too bad you don't appreciate that stuff. You ought to try it sometime."

"I'll think about it," she said. She was being sarcastic, but at least she didn't spout off about racism and colonialism. "The lady I sat next to at the rally told me the president almost always introduces a veteran. It was impressive."

Impressive. That might be the best she would come up with when it came to love of her country. Maybe she was just being polite, but he had the feeling she was building up to something.

"Do you think," she said, "I could stop in at your place and rinse the color out of my hair, wash my face?"

This surprised him. Stop at his place? Yeah, she could stop in. It was a place any man would be happy to bring a girl, even a man who lived with his sister, though he'd brought home very few. She could have asked to move in, and he'd have probably said yes.

"The black glop running down your face? Why would you want to take it off?"

She raised her hands to her cheeks, wide-eyed. "Oh, my God, I forgot all about that . . . the rain and everything. All I could think of was getting away from . . . I must look awful."

"You look like an orphan. It's cute."

She didn't react, just kept walking. "My parents don't like it. Probably a generational thing. But they're my mother and father. I indulge them."

"Really? You actually honor your father and mother? Like the Ten Commandments? There's hope for you yet." He shrugged. "But I don't mind taking you to your apartment. How far is it?"

"The university," she said, "but that's not it."

She was shaking her head. All these things of hers were digging at him, in a strange way. She kept showing a side of herself that belied the phony feminist crap she spouted. It threw him off balance. She even grabbed his bicep and moved in close to him. Under her soft hand, his arm felt like a rock, an anchor.

But she didn't seem to notice. He was afraid she would let go if she realized what she was doing. He didn't want her to let go. He hadn't had the feeling of a girl on his arm in a while.

"I'm afraid."

There it was, coming out again. The girl side of her, the side that needed somebody like him next to her. "Afraid of what?"

She stopped. They hadn't reached the sidewalk yet. They stood in the middle of the roadway. She wanted to make a point, but he had to scoot her, gently, out of the way of traffic. Here she was, calling men, husbands, and fathers, useless, when she couldn't even look both ways crossing the street. Christ, she required a babysitter.

In front of him and facing him, but still holding his arm, her eyes were full of trust. "That mob tonight. Thanks for getting me away from them. You and—what was his name, your foreman?"

"Ronan."

"Yeah. That's right. It was scary."

"That's the difference between you and me."

"What do you mean? You weren't afraid."

"I was afraid. But it's not something I mess with. I saw what was happening and I got us out of there. But you hesitated. It could've brought all of us down. You, me, even Ronan."

"How did I know you weren't some rapist, or a serial murderer?"

She had a point. But he didn't want to argue, then or now. "Fair enough. And look where you ended up. A meal, a ride home to mom and dad, and me and my truck, all in the same night. And don't worry. My sister has shampoo and whatever else you need."

CHAPTER SEVEN

"And you went to the rally exactly, why?" Michelle's question contained a faint bit of skepticism. Ricki could tell that Mike's sister had doubts about the woman she was helping out right now. Doubts any woman might have for another, especially one who had appeared on her doorstep in the company of her roommate brother.

Michelle handed Ricki the makeup remover and a cleansing cloth. Ricki began to apply the remover to the smudges. The black was everywhere. It was a mess. She turned on the faucet and wet the cloth, then began to wipe away the black. She was glad to see it all washing off.

"Curiosity, mostly," said Ricki. "Penance of a sort. I'm joining a feminist group. They expected me to go over to the other side and come back and report on it. Exactly how I chose to carry that out was up to me." She deliberately left out the part about the blog.

Talking to Mike's twin sister was way different than talking to Mike. She could be as fresh and glib as she liked with men, but something about Michelle made her button up. She'd noticed the atmosphere of the house as soon as she passed through the door. Framed family photos, some from decades long past, hung on the walls. A well-worn Bible sat on an end table. A sense of respect for tradition permeated the place. Ricki must be on her best behavior.

"Really? Here...here's a comb." Michelle rummaged through the bottom drawer in the bathroom and brought out a new one. She opened the package and handed the comb to Ricki.

"Yeah, thanks." Ricki dragged the comb through her towel-dried hair. "So, I went there with certain expectations. But I didn't find at all what I was looking for."

"And you thought you'd find . . . racists?"

Ricki stopped combing and turned away from the mirror. She spoke carefully, knowing that Michelle was studying with close intent this creature brought home by her brother. It wasn't suspicion Ricki felt coming from her, but rather caution. It would make sense that Mike and Michelle were of the same mindset. After all, they came from the same family.

"Well," she said. "At the very least, I knew I expected to disagree with most everything I saw and heard."

"And?"

"Oh, there was plenty to disagree about," she said, "but I was surprised, too."

"Turn around," said Michelle. "Let me check the back of your hair."

Ricki obeyed—she could see both of them in the mirror now. She was watching Michelle examine her hair.

"What were you surprised about?" Michelle asked.

"Mostly that it was full of genuinely nice people. Like your brother, and now you. He saved me from the middle of the riots."

"That's Mike," she said. "He thinks of other people before himself." She smoothed Ricki's hair in place. "No more green."

"Thanks," said Ricki. She checked herself closely in the mirror. "He's taking me to my parents' house. They don't like when I color my hair, so I wanted to wash it out."

"Of course." Michelle gave Ricki a look of respect. Ricki was happy she'd made a good impression. It had been a long day. She was emotionally drained by the riot and the escape from it. Michelle's approval eased her anxiety.

Mike was waiting for them when Ricki walked into the living room. She entered a bit shyly, feeling like she was presenting herself to a man on their first date. Without the colors, she looked, she knew, like a woman who would fit in at the rally. A woman who might attract the attention of the man now checking her out.

His hair was wet from the shower—curled and a little drippy. His shirt was blue instead of white but the same style. He was undeniably handsome, and his reaction at the sight of her made her breath come up short. She'd never been studied with such intensity. His head whipped up and his eyes opened wide. A burst of energy between them hit her straight in the heart. She looked away, but his gaze stayed fixed on her. She had to press her lips together and draw in her throat real tight to keep from smiling hard when she looked at him again. It didn't matter what happened between them, anyway. Ricki's priority lay with her grad program, her position in the department, and most of all, membership in the Sisterhood. Preserving the worldview took priority over a momentary flirtation. The membership tea would take place on Friday, where she would be inducted. She would not sacrifice that for any male, especially one like Mike.

"Ready to go?"

Ricki nodded. "Let me get my things."

"Sure," Mike said. "I'll wait in the truck."

CHAPTER EIGHT

I f he'd been standing up when Ricki came out into the living room, he might have fallen over. The transformation from freakish liberal to wholesome, girl-next-door was radical in and of itself. And there she was again, standing beneath the front porch light, saying goodnight to Michelle. All he wanted was to get close. Physically close. The closer the better. He scrambled from the driver's seat and sprinted around to open the door for the all-American girl who was no longer the blathering lib of thirty minutes ago. She just hadn't figured it out. Yet.

"Gosh, you look great. I mean, beautiful." He sounded like a jerk, but the words came out before he could form a coherent thought.

Daggers came out from her eyes. If they were real, they'd go straight into his heart. That meant he'd had the desired effect. He reached for the door handle.

"Don't bother." She tried to grab it first. "And don't call me that."

"Beautiful? You don't like to be thought of as beautiful? You won't even let me be nice to you?"

He laughed, even though she really knew how to piss a guy off. Any guy but him, that is. Another time, he'd have hung back, worried about what she thought, let her nail him. Now he knew better. He opened the door and chuckled.

"Nope," he said. "What I say, goes. My house, my truck, my rules."

She hoisted herself onto the seat in silence. He closed the door, softly. No slamming. She was his precious cargo, not a buddy from work.

He climbed behind the wheel, leaned over, looked straight at her. "Besides, it's my right as a toxic, white guy to tell an intersectionally challenged female she's beautiful. Especially without that crap on your face and hair."

She ignored him, fingering the stitching on the upholstery, then ran her hand over the leather. She even gave a nod of approval.

"Black. Mmmm. It's nice. Nice house. Nice truck. So, what capitalist enterprise lets you buy a vehicle of this sort? And own your own home?"

"Construction. I'm a contractor." He backed out of the driveway and put the truck in drive. "And my sister and I both own the house."

She was eyeing him differently now than on the subway, at the diner, even on the walk home. He could feel her really study him. He was glad he'd worn his work uniform to the rally. He wanted her to see him this way. He wore this every day, even on weekends. Even to presidential rallies. Button-down shirt, not a dress shirt an executive would wear to the office, but one that wouldn't look out of place under a sport coat, either. One whose sleeves he could roll up if he had to get his hands dirty. He wondered what she was thinking. He knew one thing—she took her time checking him out. He might have felt self-conscious about it, except he was enjoying busting her narrow worldview.

"What about you?"

"Teaching assistant, working on my master's degree."

"What's the master's in? Let me guess . . . gender studies?"

"That's right."

"You must have had a thousand fits at the rally; everybody sticking to their socially constructed gender roles."

She sighed. "Maybe, except for the female security. They kicked ass. But the rest of it . . . I didn't know quite what to make of it."

"The rest of what?"

"I'm not sure how to describe it, but it was different."

"Diversity? Inclusion?"

"That surprised me. But there was something more—everybody was so happy . . . and nice. Even when they found out who I was; they said welcome and we hope you enjoy it. It creeped me out. If not for the blog, I would have left early. It's got to be a cult. People just aren't that together on anything unless they've been somehow brainwashed."

He laughed out loud at that. Did she even know what she was saying? "But you didn't walk out, did you? Geez, people are happy and you get pissed."

"I'm not pissed." Except there she was, looking angry, again. Like when they first got to the diner. Like when he tried to offer her an empty seat on the subway.

He changed the subject. "Since there's nowhere in the real world to earn a living with a degree like that, you must plan to indoctrinate others in the evils of mom-and-dadhood at the university."

"I'm covered," she said, "not that I'll need it, but I've got an undergrad in business."

He laughed again. Harder this time. "Business? That's a joke, right? Wanna run mine? Then you'll find out how the real world operates. Calling in your receivables to make payroll 'cuz you've got employees with kids that need to be fed. After about two weeks of that, you'll toss that socialism shit right out the window."

"You didn't let me finish. There's more. I said I wouldn't need the business degree. Actually, I did it because my parents insisted

I get a degree that could support me financially. The master's I'm paying for on my own. But next election we'll get a president with student loan forgiveness and free college."

"Free! So you'll teach for free, right? You didn't learn much in business school, did you? Who pays your rent then?"

She sneered. This conversation was going downhill, but he was drilling into her, he could tell. And he didn't care if he pissed her off or not. She was living in Disneyland, thinking like this. And she wanted to teach others to adopt these beliefs.

"There's so much money in this country," she said, "there's no need for people to pay for health care, college, housing, anything. The government should pay for it all."

"What, how old are you, eight? Even an eight-year-old understands basic economics. 'Here's your weekly allowance, Johnny. Now, give it back to me because even though you mowed the lawn, you didn't earn it, and I'm giving it to your sister because, well, she thinks she deserves it.'"

"No, it wouldn't work that way. The government would give everyone the same amount of money, and we all spend it on the things we need." She was serious. She was looking at him, as if he should change his mind, see things her way.

"I get it. So, one of my guys working thirty-two floors up gets paid the same amount as someone on the ground teaching in a classroom or pushing pencils in an office. That's the way I see it. A guy who risks his ass every day, like a coal miner who works underground, who gets dirty, who wears himself out physically, has to retire early; all those guys should get paid the same as a preschool teacher, right?"

"After taxes, you would make the same, yes. You're rich, you can afford it."

"Rich, by how much? Richer than you? Nobody forces you to work at a shit job indoctrinating dupes who can't even think for themselves. Don't make me laugh."

She didn't respond. She just sat in the seat, fuming. "Just drop me at the corner, okay? I'll walk the rest of the way."

"What? No. Look, I'm sorry if I insulted you. But I'm delivering you safe and sound to your parents' door. I'll shut up."

"But—"

"No arguments. Just tell me how to get to your house."

They finished the ride in silence, but for Ricki's directions. When he turned into her parents' driveway, he left the truck idling and hopped out. She reached for the handle.

"I'll get the door," he said.

Of course, she let herself out, and nearly collided with him in the front of the truck.

"You just won't let anyone be nice to you, will you?"

"That has nothing to do with it."

"What is it then? That I'm a male chauvinist pig?"

She laughed at that. Finally. "Now," he said, "is that so hard?"

"It's why," she said, still laughing at him, "I wouldn't ask you to go out with me."

"Well, I make it a point not to date Nazis."

Without warning, she stepped in close, looking him right in the eye. His "female defense shield" went up. He wanted to back away, alert to danger, but instead, he went still, waiting to see what she would do. She went up on her tiptoes and softly kissed him on the mouth. They stayed together like that for several seconds. He broke away first, gently, and looked at her. Her eyes were still closed, her pale lashes lay on her cheek. She came back down and opened them, keeping her gaze to his, while he swallowed hard and tried to ignore the rushing sound in his head. She could play with a man's senses as well as any female. She had to have known what she was doing.

"You're not as smart as you think you are, are you?" she said.

"You shouldn't have done that."

"I do lots of things I shouldn't," she said. She turned and flounced away. "Have a nice life."

CHAPTER NINE

"As if that weren't enough, the white guy with the red neck
thought it would be cute to shove me into a group of these
white supremacists..."

Ricki looked up from reading aloud her rally blog post
and surveyed the large, formal living room of the Sisterhood
president, Amber Maroni. The induction ceremony had come
and gone. She was a full member. Here she was, drinking wine
spritzers on a Friday, at barely 1:00 in the afternoon. *Petra's Parlance* had received twelve thousand hits in just two days. But she
wasn't sure what bothered her more—sipping wine amidst the
formal trappings of a University Country Club mansion over-
looking the seventh fairway that was owned by the president
of the university's most radical feminist group, or her anxiety at
having publicly told such a big fat lie.

If she were being honest, Ricki would be outraged. Isn't this
what the organization constantly railed against? After all, she
had committed to a life that ran according to the trolley schedule
and all its collective merits. She bought her clothes at the Good-
will because of her budget, and because it was wrong to live any
better than the least of society. She rejected luxury in favor of

a simple and austere way of life, frugal and plain. Right now, she felt like a sad dupe. But nobody else in the room seemed to notice the hypocrisy.

The only thing that saved her conscience at the moment was the fact her story was vague enough that no person or event could be positively identified. She threw thoughtless aspersions on the crowd in general, along with some murmurings of a few invented individuals that could amount to racist insults. She included an embellished encounter with the gun club rep; and even mentioned, in disparaging tones, the guy wearing the Democrat for Trump T-shirt. If her lies were discovered, her sisters would support her. Only the end—social justice—mattered. The means were subject to interpretation.

"The white guy with the red neck drove me physically into the midst of the melee." Ricki paused before resuming her recitation of her *Petra's Parlance* blog post. *"He was a man you see everywhere. Beer gut, work pants, and steel-toed work boots. And he used those steel toes against the innocent protestors to great effect—kicking, pushing, shoving. He went crazy in the midst of the action.*

"I happened to be standing right next to him the moment he exploded. He didn't even see me. If the anti-fascists had not pulled me to safety, the redneck would simply have mowed me down. I could have been hurt." Ricki looked around at the women, now her lifetime blood sisters, all leaning toward her in silence. All eyes on her face. *"Maybe killed."*

A silent but collective intake made the room go still. And then, a unanimous burst of applause broke out.

She sat back, pleased with the reception, but she could not bask comfortably in the glory of her fellow feminists. What Ricki was really contemplating was the kiss she had given Mike. It was an impulsive act—a Judas Iscariot kiss—meant as a sign that she would soon betray his kindness in the blog post she was about to write. It worked, too. The kiss's inspiration allowed her to write the post very quickly, but her lips had not recovered. Even after three days, they felt uncomfortably warm.

"How did you know who this guy was?"

"The redneck?" She'd been trying not to think about him all morning. Actually, for the past three days she thought about little else except the feel of his mouth against hers. Its softness surprised her—yielding and eager. His desire came forth in that very instant. She held the kiss until he broke away. If he hadn't stopped when he did, she would have surrendered completely to it.

"I met him at the rally," she managed to say. "He wasn't too bright. I convinced him I was on his side, so he felt free to express himself."

"What does he do?"

"He's in construction. Runs a construction management firm. Commercial. Right now he's at the Place Four project downtown."

"You should've asked him for a date," came the wisecrack a few seats down. Everybody laughed. So did Ricki.

Across from her, perched on a richly carved mahogany chair, with needlepoint upholstery, Maya Kimball said, "Great post, Petra." The women looked at her knowingly. "And I love the lav."

Ricki smiled. She ran her fingers through her hair, tinted lavender for the occasion. "Thank you, Maya."

Today's meeting had the feeling of an elaborate banquet. An overload of emotions and images, with too much falsehood and very little truth. Conflict and guilt tore through her from the reading aloud of her blog, and the lies contained in it. Writing and posting in solitude was cleaner, easier. The cult-like reactions from her readers, from the women in the room, only brought more inner conflict and guilt. She suddenly was anxious to leave. But it wasn't over yet.

"Melissa Harding." Amber Maroni spoke again; this time her tone was sharp.

The group shifted in their chairs as Melissa stood and walked to the front of the group, an expression of slight puzzlement on her face.

CHAPTER TEN

"What's going on?" Ricki whispered to her roommate, Karen. Karen had been a member for over six months. Ricki hoped she'd fill her in. She did not like the tone of this upcoming event.

"The best part," was all Karen would say. Her hand was held out to shush Ricki's questions. Karen's face had a grin Ricki had never before seen on her roommate. The rest of the group looked slightly crazed—furrowed brows and wide-open eyes—and their postures tilted at the subject.

Melissa just looked scared.

Amber rose from her plush, velveteen navy blue armchair and stood next to Melissa, then pushed firmly down on the girl's shoulder, pushing her to her knees. She unrolled a piece of parchment and read from it.

So, this was the best part? Ricki thought that her induction was to be the meeting's highlight. But it was only the warmup for what was to come.

"For the egregious offence of having a father who is an officer of the Miami-Dade police force . . . an occupation marked by racial injustice toward marginalized communities, led by this illegitimate government, Melissa Harding is hereby censured and shunned for a period not to exceed ninety days, to commence immediately."

Melissa covered her face with both hands and pitched herself, face first, onto the floor. Ricki watched, horrified by what was happening. When the women stood in unison and turned their backs on Melissa, she did the same.

The next few minutes were excruciating. All Ricki could think of was her own father—not a police officer but an avid outdoorsman and hunter. Karen was the only one in the Sisterhood who knew of it. Would hunting in her family be grounds for shunning? She hoped she could trust Karen not to tell.

All the women turned around. Melissa was gone, somehow whisked out of their sights.

Amber acted as though nothing amiss had taken place. "Before I dismiss you, ladies," she said, "anyone is welcome to stay for cigars and whiskey in the sunroom. Otherwise, see you at next month's meeting."

In silence, the room cleared. The women picked up their bags and exited Amber's elitist nest of unearned luxury.

Out the front door, into the brightness of the day, Ricki leaned over and asked Karen, still in a whisper, "Does this happen often?"

"Oh, all the time." Karen regarded the whole thing with a shrug. "That's why it doesn't bother me. In fact, I look forward to it." She looked at Ricki and frowned. "Don't worry. It will probably happen to you sometime."

"Did Melissa know this ahead of time?"

"Nobody knows this ahead of time. We all have to come to terms with our sins. You know, do penance. The shunning is painful, but then it ends. Really, Ric, it just reminds you to be mindful of your privilege. This organization isn't open to everyone, you know."

She and Karen caught a ride to the trolley line then rode the two stops home. Karen chatted happily about the meeting. Ricki, circumspect, couldn't get out of her mind the bizarre image of

Melissa, on her knees, a look on her face like she wanted to die. Maybe it was the wine, making her feel tipsy and off kilter. Maybe it was the giant lie of the blog post; her fear of being discovered that her own father hunted the food on the family table. The fact that Ricki did not hunt, had no desire to, and had recently given up eating meat, might not matter in this case. And how would the Sisterhood even find out? That might be the most disturbing question of all.

They entered the building. Karen took the elevator to their apartment while Ricki stopped to collect the mail.

"Hey there, Miss Petra."

She forgave Jack, the building super, for calling her Miss, maybe because he used her secret pen name Petra. It had become a joke between them.

"Hey, Jack."

She locked the mailbox and fished through the stack. Jack wore his usual work belt laden with tools and carried a fiberglass stepladder. She smiled at him, ready for a bit of tit for tat.

Jack's face had a funny look. Not joking, not his usual cheerful self.

"I read your blog post."

"Oh?" She wanted to sound casual, but Jack's lack of joking and cheer had her on edge.

Jack was looking at the floor, not at her, shaking his head. "Not cool, Petra, not cool."

"What do you mean?" Her stomach bounced a little as she waited to hear him out. She fiddled with the stack of envelopes in her hand.

Jack had read her writing before, and almost always disagreed. He always made sure to let her know, too, where he thought she was wrong. It never put a strain between them, probably because their acquaintance was so casual that politics wasn't really an issue. But today, even before he began to talk, she felt his judgement. Her defenses rose.

"You, you talked about that rally the other day, right?"

She nodded, not liking the direction this conversation was going.

"I hate to say this, I really do. You and me, we always got along, right? But Miss Petra, you're full of it. And you have to know it. I was there. I was at that rally. None of that happened. Look at me, I'm a Black man. If anybody saw white supremacists—" Jack stuck his head out the backdoor of the building and spat into a patch of lawn, "—that would be me, and I'll tell you for a fact that stuff you wrote? Bullshit. All of it."

Jack picked up the ladder and headed toward the back of the building, on to whatever task came next on his endless list. Just before he reached the corner, he turned back.

"You wrote a big lie. And innocent people are out there; and your group and the people like them just want to destroy those good, innocent people."

Ricki stared after Jack. She couldn't think of anything to say. But she was angry. Angry because someone who spent his days as a janitor—dared to call her out. Dishonesty had nothing to do with it. The people at the rally were guilty of all the injustice she could name, and she could name a lot.

And Jack, a man of color, one of the oppressed, should know better. After all, she wrote the column on behalf of him and all the marginalized peoples of the world; the people forgotten and despised by this president. And here he defended the hate. She couldn't understand it.

Except it stung. Because she had lied. And she resented having to face the truth of what she had done, and nothing she said to him would change that fact. And that lie had brought her exactly what she hoped for: membership in the Sisterhood, and a story that was now going viral. She—as *Petra's Parlance*—had become famous in less than twenty-four hours.

Yes, she had made up every bit of that post. There was nothing truthful about it. But that was beside the point because the point was to equal the imbalance in the scales of justice. And this was the way, and it was a very good way, she had chosen to go about it. The women today would applaud her courage—spread the story far and wide. It would earn her much acclaim in her world, no matter how small.

As soon as she reached her apartment, she fired up her laptop, ready to scroll through and answer the dozens, by now perhaps hundreds, of emails and comments she knew would be waiting. She could answer each one. She would. She set to work. An hour later came a buzz on her phone—her mom, texting, *"Come home ASAP. We need to talk."*

CHAPTER ELEVEN

Trolley ridership was light this afternoon, but Ricki mostly thought about the last time she saw Mike and what it felt like when he looked at her in his living room after she'd washed her hair and taken off the black makeup. And then there was that kiss. Not even her parents' summons could cool that lingering heat. So strange it would stay there for three days, through the writing and posting of her blog; the weird triumph of today's induction into the Sisterhood; even override the unease of Melissa Harding's shunning, and Jack's failed attempts to shame her.

And ever since she'd impulsively put that kiss on Mike's face, she'd wondered what her life would be like to have a guy—a lover, not a friend. Even, heaven forbid, a husband. She must be getting older or getting soft. Either way, Mike didn't really enter into that picture. He had only been the catalyst for this new notion of "boyfriend." Mike could never pass the test of "right guy" for Ricki, and the reasons were so obvious she did not even need to list them. Although, now that she thought of it, she couldn't picture Mr. Right, either. She dropped the idea. She focused, instead, on the turn her life had taken. The blog post that was a lie now surpassed fifteen thousand hits—she was fast becoming a public figure. She'd been booked on a local podcast, scheduled for 8:00 p.m. tonight. A growing number of "woke folks" on her side wanted eagerly to hear about her adventures in racist land. As much as she looked forward to getting her long-awaited tattoo tomorrow, this new phase held a promise for Ricki she never could have foreseen. It was a chance to spread the woke view of the world. She tamped down the nagging uncertainty dredged up by Amber's hypocrisy and Jack's calling out of her dishonesty and walked the short distance from the trolley to her parents' house ready to meet the challenges of a high-visibility future.

CHAPTER TWELVE

Four blocks later, when she turned the corner to her parents' street, she was hit with a shock that brought out the full force of the truth of what she had been trying to hide from herself, and the world. In the driveway of her parents' home sat Mike's beefy, very black, super-cab pickup truck. It was unmistakable.

Her stomach bottomed out at the sight. He would be inside now, sitting in her parents' living room; they looking at him, and he looking back at them. Whatever, she wondered, were they talking about? She pulled out her phone to check the time. An hour since she'd received the summons from her parents. Two hours since Jack's admonishment in the building lobby. Three hours since the triumph at the induction tea. Two days since the blog post appeared. Not possible for all this to be related. Or was it? The guilt she felt at this moment began to unravel her inner story, telling herself to justify the lie that was careening through the blogosphere even now.

In the front room sat her mother and father, with grave faces. On the sofa sat Mike, awkward and uncomfortable with his hands folded in his lap, tapping the pads of his thumbs together.

He looked at her as though she were something he could chew up and spit out.

"Hello." She kept her face mild as she addressed her parents. "Is this about your trip next week?" She could think of nothing else to say to ease the strangeness.

Her father cleared his throat and declined to address her question. Ominous.

"We've been talking to Mike." He and Mike both nodded, men's curt nods of acknowledgement. Masculine, purposeful. "And now we'd like to talk to you."

One chair that anchored the corner of the plush Oriental carpet remained vacant. It was a simple parlor chair, the type meant to keep people from staying too long. Ricki sat and waited. Her mother held up a sheet of paper, with typing. "Did you write this?"

Her anger growing by the minute, Ricki took the page. It was like middle school all over again, when she'd been busted for some transgression or other. Busted by the people she most cared about. She wasn't certain if Mike belonged in the "cared about" category. But he was a nice man, anyway, and she'd used him under false pretenses for her own gain. And all he'd been to her was a decent human being. Even more, he'd gone out of his way for her; kept her from harm when he didn't even know who she was. Saved her from a savage mob; fed her, taken her into his home; and seen her safely back to this house. Right now, she wished like hell she wasn't thinking these thoughts.

"Mike came by an hour ago," her father said. "It seems this writing—this *Petra's Parlance*, as you call it—has caused him quite a bit of trouble."

"My job site!" Mike broke in. Ricki noticed he was dressed in the same white shirt and work pants as the rally. His boots, as heavy and lumbering as before, held him firmly in place. Or maybe his feet were just large.

He glowered beneath bushy brows. "It's crawling with punks—" he pointed to the paper in her hand. The ones who "saved" you from me—in that piece of crap fiction. You lied! You lied about me, about everyone, about the whole rally. I kept you from getting hurt! We ate together at the diner, had coffee. I brought you here, to your parents' house because you didn't feel safe going back to your apartment."

Ricki's mom looked as if she wanted to cry; her father's face was a mix of anger and disbelief. She couldn't look at Mike at all. Just hearing his words, accusing, as if she were the cause of this, was bad enough. But she wondered something, too—how had Mike been outed?

"I'm sorry," she was stumbling, trying to say the right thing; trying to understand the situation. "I never meant for this to happen to you. I made sure to keep anything out of that blog post that might get you, or anyone else, identified."

Mike walked over to her and showed her his phone. "Look," he said. "Here is my business." On the screen was video of a mob of black-clad young males blocking an access point in a construction site fence.

Jack, the building super, had just called her out for lying. Now, her parents and Mike, along with them, were confronting her with the truth. She wished she didn't care. She couldn't bear, at this moment and before these people, to admit she'd done wrong, even though it was staring her in the face. They simply didn't understand what was at stake. They could all go to hell.

She stood up. "So I suppose it's my fault you happen to be on the wrong side?"

Mike shoved the phone into his pocket. "Wrong side? I treat you with kindness, you get me doxxed, and I'm on the wrong side?"

Ricki's father broke in, "If you deliberately besmirched Mike's reputation . . . that's evil, Ricki. I'll say it. It's evil."

"But nobody was supposed to know! I didn't mean for this to get out!"

Ricki sat down as she skimmed the page her mother handed her, looking for something that would have caused Mike to be doxxed, even though she knew by heart nothing was in there. She wished she had stayed back in Amber's living room, puffing a cigar and sipping whiskey among the carefully styled bookshelves and the potted palms. It wouldn't have erased the problem, but at least she could have pleaded inebriation to her parents and delayed this confrontation. And then she remembered—she mentioned out loud the name of Mike's job site at the tea. Somebody, likely Amber Maroni, turned it over to the powers that be on the left. Mobilization had happened instantly. It was her own big mouth that outed him—the carelessness caused by the necessity to keep her facts straight. When she looked at Mike, she saw in herself the very worst in human nature. And nothing she did, ever, could make up for good intentions. Her father was right. She'd deliberately smeared a good man; a good movement; good people, even a good president who she thought she despised. He'd called it evil—tough to swallow. So, in this living room she was evil. And yet, back at Amber's, she had the approval, the "attagirls," of the Sisterhood. And of her readers. And to them, the lie would not matter, as long as she maintained it. That would be her choice to make, then. Accept the truth and try to make it right, or double down on her lies.

"Mike is the nicest young man, Ricki. He knocked on the door this morning. He was very polite. He apologized for bothering us. He told us right away who he was and why he'd come to the house."

Ricki's mother stared at her with a hardness she'd never before seen. It felt worse, even, than when she'd broke curfew in high school. But she wasn't fifteen anymore. She was ten years older. In high school, she felt unjustly accused. She was the sinner. They stood in judgement. It was the same now, except now, the consequences were far greater. She'd never, ever considered this would happen. And it was too late to prevent the damage done to Mike. His business. His reputation. His workplace.

A tiny buzz came from Mike's phone. "Excuse me." He fished it from his pocket, scanned the screen, then keyed in some letters and stood up. "Sorry, but I've got to go. That was my foreman. The police are arriving on scene; they'll want to talk to me."

He shook hands with Ricki's mom and dad. "Frank, Emma, I can't thank you enough for your kindness."

Ricki's father spoke. "And thank you, Mike, for watching over Ricki at the rally. We are so sorry this had to happen."

Mike turned and faced Ricki. "I've got to go try and undo some of the damage."

As he walked to the front door, she jumped from her chair and caught up with him in two strides. "Wait!"

Mike turned back in silence. He fiddled with his hands in his jacket pockets. She could hear the jingle of keys.

"What can I do to make it up? Mike," she said, plaintively. "I want to make it up."

He looked at her, his face nearly white. "Make it up?" He shook his head as he walked out of the house without replying.

She didn't want it to end this way. She couldn't let him leave, with no resolution. She had to try to fix it, even though she didn't know what that would be.

She caught up to him as he unlocked his truck door and opened it. "I'm so sorry, Mike. I know how this happened and it's my fault. I accidentally said the name of your job site aloud during my meeting today. Someone did the research and doxxed you. I'm so sorry. I never thought this would happen."

He gave her a look. "Yeah, you never thought. That much is true," he said. He took a revolver from the console compartment of his truck, opened the cylinder to check it for rounds, then snapped it shut and secured it to a bracket under his dashboard.

"What are you doing?" she said.

"When you get threats to your life," he said, "you need a way to defend yourself, and you need to keep it handy."

"Please be careful." She didn't know what else to say.

He spoke through clenched teeth. "Why don't you stop talking and start doing—something good instead of destroying?"

He climbed in his cab and started the engine. Ricki could only watch as he backed slowly from the driveway and took off down the street.

The house was quiet when she came back inside. She tiptoed into the basement, miserable. She didn't want to see or talk to anyone. Mike was a generous and decent man, who went out of his way to protect a perfect stranger when that perfect stranger was oblivious to the dangers she faced; and then that perfect stranger had used the excuse of being a perfect stranger to destroy the livelihood, and reputation, of the generous and decent man. And why? For acceptance into a club of ungrateful hypocrites who wanted to destroy all that was good about people and society. And destroy men, too. Especially men. Well, Ricki had turned into the poster child of using lies to destroy innocent people. And for all its lofty intentions, there was not a shred of good about it.

Before he left her parents' house, Mike had said to stop talking and do something good instead of destructive. He was right. Her apologies, her protests, her arguments were so weak in the face of his good acts. Words meant nothing. Except all she had were words. But words could be accompanied by an act. A blog post had destroyed a good man's reputation. Maybe a blog post could help to overcome that destruction. In one brief moment, Ricki threw off the false narrative of everything she'd once thought brave and true and right. In the hopes of salvaging one good thing from this disaster, she decided to sacrifice everything she thought important that had proven to be false.

She sat down in the basement room that served as her back-at-home quarters and fired up the desktop computer. Then she began to type. The words came slowly at first, then faster. After thirty minutes, she went back to reread what she had written. Her first paragraph stunned her.

"I've told you the story of the rally I attended. That story was a lie. I now give you the story that is the whole truth, the entire truth. It begins with a man who lives by the rule "Ladies First," and he lives every word of that. I know his rule firsthand, for he practiced it with me, even though my own acts in the face of his kindness were far from ladylike.

As I grew into adulthood, I quashed the dream of every little girl who wants to marry her handsome prince. It was silly. It was all a result of centuries of white male oppression and privilege. Well, I'm here to tell you that handsome princes do exist. I met one.

Let me tell you about him, and how he saved me from the ravages of a violent, anti-fascist mob after the rally; and how he saved me from being completely taken over by the raving lunacy of what we call feminism today. I renounce that. And I'm here to tell you why . . .

CHAPTER THIRTEEN

After spending the night at her parents' house, Ricki woke up early and went out to run errands. Her tattoo appointment was later today. She planned to drop off her supplies at her apartment, pack a bag, pick up the tattoo money, and head back to her parents until her tattoo session.

As she approached the corner of the street where her apartment house stood, Ricki heard the chants and shouts, all of it angry. Staying in the shade of the Larkspur Avenue trees, her neighborhood's only leafy block, she stopped. She crept alongside the wall of the corner drugstore, then peeked around the corner. The noise came from the front of her apartment building.

A mob, looking and sounding like the rioters that caused the mayhem at the rally, was stationed in front. There were more than she could count—a pieced-together mass of humans, flanked by sign-carriers, many of them female. Were any of them members of her Sisterhood, she wondered. Sometimes, she had participated in acts of protest when right wingers spewed particularly vicious hate speech. Now she appeared to be a target of the same tactics. Her *mea culpa* post, as she called it, was long and rambling. She came clean on everything—renouncing her beliefs, which she called "a state of astonishing incoherence," and especially renouncing her treatment of Mike. So the mob, once attacking the rallygoers, once attacking Mike the redneck, had set itself upon her.

The rioters wore black hoods and masks. Some carried bats; some slapped weapons-grade bike locks against their thighs. She imagined; no, she knew for a fact, that some carried knives beneath their shirts. She flattened herself against the wall and scooted back out of sight.

Never before had she given a second thought to the protests of anti-fascist groups against the injustices of the alt-right. But this group, probably the same one protesting Mike's job site, was now out to get her. And a new wave of fear hit as, for the second time in one week, her physical safety at the hand of leftist thugs was at risk.

She checked the time. In four hours, she was due for her tattoo session. She was carrying supplies and a bag of ice. She needed to drop off the items, pick up the money for the tattoo artist, plus school materials for the upcoming week, and hole up at her parents' house while they were gone on vacation, where she could nurse her tattoo wounds in peace.

She dialed Karen's number. Karen picked up immediately.

"Ricki!" Karen sounded frantic.

"Karen, what's going on? There's a mob in front of the house. I'm at the drugstore, outside. Is there any way to get in the building?"

"You can try the service entrance, but there are spotters out there, Ricki. I looked."

"But I need to get in." She paused as the gravity set in. "They might try to kill me."

"Can you blame them?"

"What?"

"Look, Ricki. There's a sign out there. I don't know if you saw it. I'm looking at it now. It says "Petra the Fascist." That sums it up, Ricki. It's what you are."

She was firmly in her new world, and hearing the old words being hurled at her. She knew them, knew them well. But they no longer made sense. The new readership, tripled in just twenty-four hours, all of whom celebrated Ricki-as-Petra's lies, now sought to bludgeon her for writing the truth. She'd become one of them. One of Mike, her family, the rallygoers, even one of the president's supporters.

"Ricki, are you still there?"

"Yes, I'm here. Karen, my tattoo session is in four hours. I need to get in and get my things. And my money's in there, too."

"Things? Money? Ricki, you wrote a blog post yesterday full of the most vile hate I've ever read. You committed violence against these people, who only want to right the wrongs of the oppressor against the marginalized. And you've put the rest of the neighborhood in danger. As soon as this is over, I'm leaving, finding another place to live. This friendship is over. Oh, and I called Amber Maroni and thanked her for outing you. She told me to tell you your membership in the Sisterhood is hereby revoked."

Karen hung up. Ricki looked at her dark phone screen. The mob was still outside, quieter now, but she doubted they'd be leaving anytime soon. She peeked around the corner again. If anything, the numbers had grown. She needed a plan.

She could cancel her tattoo session, but she would not give the mob that power. She would not let them have even one small victory. For years she'd planned and saved for this day. She would not change it. But keeping her appointment meant that she must face the mob. And to Ricki, facing the mob meant more than making her way through an angry, violent crowd. Facing the mob meant cleansing the evil that once lurked in her soul. Facing the mob meant rekindling the values she'd been raised with and had recently found in a man called Mike. And that man called Mike wore steel-toed boots and could break through walls of violent thugs. She prayed, for the first time in a long time, he would apply his grandfather's rules to her now, despite his anger, if she asked him to. She brought out her phone, found his number and hit dial.

"Redway, Mike."

Her hands shook when she heard his voice. She sank against the wall but didn't hesitate.

"Mike, it's Ricki."

Pause. Silence.

"Yeah." Gruff. Terse. She was getting clobbered from all sides today. But Mike was her only hope to salvage this important day. He was "ladies first," by his own admission, all the time. His grandfather had made certain of it. Even though she didn't feel like a lady at the moment, she could fix it.

"There's a mob outside my apartment. I need help."

"Call your roommate."

"She hung up on me."

"Oh, yeah?" Finally, some animation came into his voice.

"She won't help. Can't help. Not with that mob."

"Call your mom and dad. I'm busy right now."

"They left for vacation."

"I could use a vacation myself. Look, what do you want from me? I'm in the middle of a job. I thought you were a supplier calling me back."

"No!" The sobs building up were becoming harder and harder to hold in. Tattoo or no tattoo, she had to get into her apartment. She was weighed down with supplies and holding a melting bag of ice. "I've got to get in there. I'm afraid I'll get hurt."

"A mob. Again."

"Yes! They're after me." She shouted, nearly hysterical, needing to reach that sweet gallantry from the night they met. "I wrote another blog post after you left yesterday. I told the truth, the real story. The new story went viral, too. Only now the mob is against me." Ricki felt smaller in size with every plea she uttered.

"What do you want me to do?"

"Take me through the crowd; help me get into my apartment."

"Well, I can't leave until I take delivery on some materials here." Pause. "Look, I'm really busy. You'll have to find another way to do it."

She resorted to tears. The only thing she had left. "Please, Mike." She pushed out the words between sobs. "I'm afraid. I need your help."

It worked. He was silent. She hated herself for it, but the sobs were real; every tear was real. There was no faking this helpless and female self.

"Wait a second. Let me call you back. Can you wait where you're at?"

The fear subsided. He would come and help her, after all. "Yes." Her voice came out tiny, the way she felt at the moment.

Less than a minute passed before he called back. "I just talked to Michelle. She's at the house. Go there and wait. I'll be there as soon as I can."

He hung up.

She had no choice but to do what he told her. For the second time, she was under his protection. It was a feeling she could get used to. And she wished for more of it. For more of him. She emptied the bag of ice onto a sidewalk planter with a live oak tree and headed back to the trolley station.

CHAPTER FOURTEEN

When Michelle answered the door, Ricki made it a point to study her features, looking for resemblance. She saw enough to peg them as siblings. Eyes, mouth, facial expressions. Michelle tucked her hair behind her ears and stepped aside.

"Come on in."

The door closed. An air of expectation hung about the room. Ricki supposed she should speak.

"Thanks for letting me come." She felt foolish. Here she was, seeking refuge from the sister of the man she called a racist.

"Sure. What's going on?"

"There's a mob outside my building."

"A mob. What sort of mob?"

"Do you mind if I sit?"

Michelle had to be angry. And Ricki could not blame her. Ricki had an older brother, Carl. What if some babe did that to him, even though he was a married man with kids? The thought alone made her angry.

Michelle waved her hand. "Of course. Sorry."

Ricki sat. She'd worn her most conservative clothes today—a white, button-down blouse tucked into her ankle length jeans, paired with black patent-leather ballet flats that she kept at her parents' house. Her days of ripped jeans and black nails and tinted hair were now in the past.

Michelle looked down at her own baggy sweatshirt and pajama bottoms before taking one end of the couch and tucking her feet underneath her.

"Sorry, I'm cleaning closets."

Ricki shrugged. She really did not know what to say. She looked around. "How long have you guys lived here?"

"Ten years? Maybe more. We bought it during college. Better than dorm living."

"It's very nice." She decided to try and make amends with Michelle. "I'm sure you know about what happened to Mike—my fault, of course."

Michelle nodded. "At his job site?"

"I named him in a blog post I wrote. I was careful not to include any info that could identify him. But I let slip the name of his job site at the new member tea yesterday, and somebody doxxed him. Wait, let me back up."

Ricki told the rally story from the very beginning. She told Michelle of Mike blocking the onrush of riders so she could board the trolley car; how the people at the rally were so different than what she expected—the man at the gun club exhibit; the man in the Democrats for Trump T-shirt; how Mike had kept her out of trouble when the riot broke out later; taking her to the diner for food; then here, to this house, where she met Michelle. The tea party she later attended where she accidentally outed Mike's identity.

"And you were kind and helped me," she said, "even though I was so . . . different."

"Different, how?"

"My looks, for one thing. And my politics."

Michelle nodded. "Your politics are your business. Besides, I respected that you were willing to go to the other side. And when you said that you didn't want to wear those colors to your parents' house, I knew you were a good person."

"Thank you," said Ricki. She did not deserve Michelle's praise. "But then I betrayed you, Mike, and my family. I wrote the post about the rally—a total lie."

"Why did you do it?"

"To increase my readership. And to get into a feminist sorority I wanted membership in."

Ricki laughed to herself. "It seems so absurd now. Well, that's over with, anyway. The president rescinded my membership this morning. It only lasted twenty-four hours."

"Ah, feminism," said Michelle. Was Michelle being sarcastic, contemptuous, both, neither? Ricki did not know how to respond. Feminism was not part of Michelle's lexicon, though it had formed Ricki's entire worldview. But Michelle was certainly a strong woman who deserved respect. Michelle's life, and the lives of say, her rally seatmates, maybe all the women who voted for Trump over Hillary, was just as full, independent, and active as hers.

"And Mike was just being polite. He told me his grandfather—"

"Taught him to treat ladies with respect."

"I haven't acted much like a lady."

"And the post went viral, and Mike was in it, and he got doxxed," said Michelle. "Excuse me." She rose and adjusted the thermostat, then she disappeared into the kitchen. Ricki looked around the comfortable living room. Though simple, it was furnished far more luxuriously than her apartment. Nothing looked expensive or brand new. It spoke more of cast-offs from the family den. The couch where she and Michelle sat matched the easy chair, the one where Mike was sitting the other night when she walked into the living room and felt that unmistakable zing between them. A pair of lamps and end tables completed the ensemble. The room was inviting and cozy without being pretentious.

Ricki felt a little envious, knowing that Mike and Michelle were able to afford their own condo. It made so much sense to build equity in a home. Amber was a hypocrite, a leftist steeped in country club luxury. She did not follow her own rules that she imposed on others. Ricki did, at one time, follow those rules—secondhand clothing; mass transit; no more than two pairs of shoes. But Mike and Michelle lived their values, too, without apology. It was the lifestyle of her own parents and probably Mike's family, too. All had the same values in common—love America, work hard, be prosperous, help others. She'd made the choice just yesterday, knowing the damage she caused to Mike, and to his business, that she would once again live those values for herself. They would form the basis for this new life of hers.

Michelle returned with cheese and crackers and iced tea on a tray. Ricki helped herself to a glass of tea then took a slice of cheese and put it on a cracker.

"It was a terrible thing I did." She took a sip of tea and looked up at Michelle from over the rim of her glass. "I'm so sorry."

Michelle shrugged and checked her watch. "It will be over soon. Mike has good security. It isn't his first scrape with haters of America and capitalism."

"He came to my parents' house, yesterday. Right after the new member tea. Confronted me. I apologized. But it took him confronting me to realize I'd done something terrible. Maybe unforgiveable."

At the word "unforgiveable" Ricki knew right away she wanted Mike's forgiveness. It had to be why she couldn't let go of him. Why she'd thought to call him when she got in trouble with the mob. She'd wanted the protection she knew he'd give her if she asked; more than that, she felt the need to see him again. Maybe, if he saw her again, she'd be forgiven, and she could forgive herself. The new blog post had been a start.

"After he left my parents' house yesterday, I wrote a new blog post. I couldn't just let the original post stand. Mike told me I should stop talking and do something good." She gave a small smile. Michelle smiled back.

"Mike's like that," said Michelle. "He likes to see action; he's not a man of words."

"I told the truth. I rejected the false values, the hate, the intolerance. I'm not part of that scene anymore."

"And when you go against those people, they make you pay."

"That's right."

Michelle twisted her fingers, rested them under her chin. "So, where do you go from here?"

"My apartment, to get some things, when Mike gets here. I'm staying at my parents' while they're away for a few days. This afternoon I have a session scheduled at the tattoo parlor. My money is at my apartment."

Ricki looked at her phone. Less than an hour had passed since Mike had told her to come here and wait. How funny that it gave her such a feeling of comfort to know he would soon be here, to help her. She wished she could feel this way, always. Minus the awful insecurity caused by her misdeed. She wondered if there might be any way to get him to see her in a different light.

"What I meant was, your life, where in your life are you going?" Michelle asked.

"Oh, that." Ricki laughed. "Reading, for starters, while I'm at my parents' house nursing my tattoo. I need a new perspective on things, and there's a lot to learn. There's clarity on this side—it's not muddled like over there. There's a conservative capitalist in me ready to show itself. I'm excited for it."

"But you still want the tattoo?"

"Yes. I've wanted that since I was a kid. One doesn't have anything to do with the other."

"What tattoo parlor are you using?" Michelle seemed intrigued by the idea.

"Covington Tattoo Group."

"So, this blog post of yours, can I read it?"

"Sure. It's my *mea culpa* post. But why do you want to read it?"

"I'm curious." Michelle seemed genuinely friendly. Ricki had an innate trust in her. "I'm fascinated by your thinking."

"You mean, about this change in my political views?"

"I don't often meet people who reject their political beliefs, especially someone on the left."

"Oh, you mean getting red-pilled?" She laughed at herself for using the term. "I saw it on one of the signs in front of my apartment this morning. It wasn't meant as a compliment."

"Well, it's what happens, isn't it?"

Ricki nods. "It's exactly what happens. I couldn't ignore the hypocrisy anymore."

"The side that calls itself the tolerant?"

"You got it." Ricki walked to the corner desk. "Okay, fire up your computer. You can meet the new Petra."

They were in the midst of reading the Mike-as-Ricki's-Hero part of the blog, when Mike walked through the front door. He paid no attention to the reading. He had other things on his mind. Assured and unafraid, he immediately took charge.

"I've got one of the guys over there now scoping out the situation. They're basically the same punks as the ones that showed up at Place Four." He stared at Ricki, then looked away. Her heartbeat rose at the sight of him, then sank at his coldness. It was like talking through a plexiglass barrier.

"Michelle, stay here and be on alert in case I need you."

Michelle nodded. "I'm just cleaning closets. I'll keep my phone on me."

"I've got some of the BlackFire crew outside. They're going to follow us over there. Ronan's driving my truck." Finally, he spoke to Ricki. "You ready to go? I'll explain how we're handling this on the way over."

She nodded. "Sure, I'm ready. But what's BlackFire?"

His reply was clipped. "A private security firm I contract with. They fill in where the police leave off."

Ricki wasn't sure about all this planning. It sounded, and felt, like some kind of precision military op. She hesitated.

"They're pros," said Mike, seeing her hesitate. "They know this business, and they know the law. They do thugs. Besides, they answer to me."

So, all she was required to do was ride along and collect her stuff. Mike would do the rest. The secure feeling returned. As they reached the front door, Mike's phone rang.

"Yeah? Did they say when they'd get there?" Mike snorted. "Okay, well, we'll do the best we can."

He put his phone away.

"Police aren't really interested. They said they'd send someone over to take a look but if they aren't blocking car or pedestrian traffic, they can't do anything."

"But what if they're threatening people?" asked Ricki.

Mike gave her a long look, as though she should understand what was a very basic fact.

"That all depends on whose side they're on."

CHAPTER FIFTEEN

Evidently Jack, the super, had been alerted by Mike's look-out. He was waiting for them at the back entrance. He held the door open while Mike ushered Ricki inside, then locked it.

"I'll wait here until you leave," he said.

The BlackFire guys had quietly infiltrated the group in front. At the right time, they would distract the mob so Mike and Ricki could escape out the back of the building. Ricki took Mike up to her floor in the elevator.

"That was easy." She turned the key in the lock and let them in. A faint musty odor hung in the air.

"Once they find out we're here," said Mike, "the hard part will be making it out. Alive."

Ricki hoped he was exaggerating. She walked to the living room window and drew back the curtains.

Karen poked her head out her bedroom door. "Are they still out there?" She saw Mike and stepped out. "Oh, I didn't know you brought someone."

Ricki said, "Karen, this is Mike. Mike, this is Karen, my room-mate. And yeah, they're still out there."

"Nice to meet you." Karen cast a doubtful glance at Mike, but she was on her best behavior. "Excuse me. I'm going back in. Ricki, I'll be leaving either later today or tomorrow. I'm moving in with Carla and Lorraine. You can get hold of me there."

"Sure, Karen. We'll work it out." Ricki nodded. Her old life was falling away quickly. The hate and rage she once carried were gone. Her club membership and best friend had both vaporized in a few hours. But instead of feeling dragged down by it, she felt liberated. And it had all been done without a gut-wrenching decision to move out; or having to work up the courage to quit that useless club. A flash of what she would do about her teaching job and master's degree came and went. She would deal with that later.

Mike looked out the window. "I don't see so many punks. But you can see my guys down there. Come take a look."

Ricki looked at the men Mike pointed out. They didn't wear uniforms or matching clothing at all, like the detail at the rally. Instead, they wore T-shirts and jeans or cargo pants and blended in with the crowd.

He turned to Ricki. "Go collect your things. I'm going to call down and see what it looks like in back."

Ricki grabbed her suitcase from her closet shelf. Days ago, she might have joined the protesters outside, tried to obstruct the police. She was certain that the anti-fascist thugs downstairs intended to do the same thing if the police would even come out to check. It had never occurred to her she might be watched by plainclothes police or private security. Would the thugs on the street below be aware? She suddenly felt enormous respect for Mike, taking care of his employees and securing their job sites.

Ricki threw in a pair of jeans and two plaid shirts along with socks and underwear. Her briefcase with school materials was already full of the papers and books she needed. She packed her sweetest object last. An envelope filled with cash she had saved up over several years. It would go to her tattoo artist, Jenna, this afternoon. She placed it carefully on top of her clothes, then zipped the case closed.

In the living room, Mike reached for Ricki's bags. "I can take this one." She held up her briefcase. "It's not heavy."

He snatched it away. "No," he said. He threw the briefcase strap over one shoulder as he looked her square on. She knew by the way he said it that he had other things on his mind besides the bulk of her belongings. He picked up the suitcase.

"Ronan's waiting out back with the truck. Most of the mob is still out front, but a few lookouts are stationed in back. That's where we have to go. But it buys us a little time. We'll go as fast as we can. Stay with me. We'll do fine. Ready?"

"Okay," said Ricki.

The elevator ride down to the lobby was quiet. Ricki tried to ignore the tension. The fear was like escaping the mob after the rally, but this time she was their sole target.

Mike stepped off the elevator first. He used his body and the suitcases to shield Ricki from the view of the crowd through the glass front doors. Jack waited at the back. He signaled an all-clear to Mike, who led Ricki by the hand through the doors. Once outside, he walked swiftly to avoid attention, tugging her along behind him. The lookouts alerted their cohorts in front, but up ahead, not twenty yards from them, sat Ronan behind the wheel of Mike's idling truck.

Mike threw open the back door of the cab and tossed the bags inside. Then he picked up Ricki, who was already reaching for a handhold, and boosted her in. She flopped onto the seat, feeling like a piece of luggage herself, and scooted quickly to the other side. Mike scrambled in. Before he could shut the door, Ronan stepped on the gas. He had the truck moving, just as the lookouts were reaching for the door handles. One, already on the bumper of the truck bed, was flung off backwards when Ronan hit the gas. At the rear of the building, the black-clad crowd was growing, but it was too late. The teamwork of Mike, Ronan, and BlackFire had thwarted the gang.

She looked at Mike. He was looking back at her, his mouth a grim line. He had saved her. He had saved them both, again.

CHAPTER SIXTEEN

"Can I ever see you again?"

They sat in the driveway of her parents' house. He'd driven her here in silence, after the exit from her apartment building. Ronan rode back to the job site with the BlackFire crew once they all arrived at the meeting place away from the melee.

Ricki hadn't spoken, either. Only now could she say something; when their time together was up; when he hadn't said anything; when the tension compelled her to speak. She'd never before spoken to a man in this way. But she had to try. She had to know.

Mike only shook his head, staring out the windshield, rubbing his thumb over the steering wheel. He didn't take the bait.

"We don't belong together. We're too different." He turned and faced her, finally. She tried her best not to appear too hurt. "I'm an old-fashioned guy. I can't do it your way. Guys ask girls; girls don't ask guys."

He was right. So far, she'd done all the wrong things. At least until she wrote the *mea culpa* blog. But, when he showed up to help her today, it had given her hope. Plus, she meant every word she'd written. He was the kind of man she would marry. She must be in love with him if she was able to think about him that way. If he would not return the feelings, she'd be devastated.

"Haven't I apologized enough? I wrote that blog post. It's why that crowd was in front of my building. I wanted to make it up to you. It was the only way I knew how."

She wasn't explaining herself well at all; at least, not well enough to get through to him.

He kept staring out the windshield. "I came to get you this morning—consider that my forgiveness. That will have to be enough. I promised myself I would never let a girl make a fool out of me. And you made a fool of me."

He reached down and turned the key, started the truck. "You'd better go. I've got to be somewhere."

She touched his arm. "Mike, please, listen."

He pulled his arm away and shot a look at her, filled with fire. "No. I don't want to listen. I've got nothing to say to you."

Ricki flounced out of the cab and opened the back door to retrieve her belongings. He did not even come around to help her, the grandfatherly, gentlemanly gesture that she knew to be him. He only sat in the driver's seat, staring down into his lap, while the engine rumbled its urgency to be on the road.

Ricki slammed the door and walked up the front walk as Mike took off down the street. He didn't even wait to leave until she was safely inside. That feeling of comfort that had started to fit like a favorite jacket went away. She would have to get used to being without it.

And, as she entered the house and shut the door behind her, hope, the kind of hope that allowed her to fall in love with a good man with old-fashioned values, died.

CHAPTER SEVENTEEN

Michelle was still home, rummaging through the closets, when he walked in. He heard muffled grunts, and the sound of stuff being shoved aside.

"Hey, come here and help, would you?"

Michelle was struggling with a too-big box crammed onto a too-high shelf. "Did everything go okay at Ricki's place?"

"Yeah, fine," he said. "Don't you have somewhere to go?" Mike didn't like his mood just now. He certainly didn't want to be sharing it with her.

"Here, take this box and no, I don't."

"Where do you want me to put it?"

"On the dining room table. I need to sort through it."

He hoisted the box through the living room and into the dining room.

"What's in it?"

Michelle faced him and put her hands on her hips. "It's grandma's old china. I want to make an arrangement of her plates on the kitchen wall." She narrowed her eyes and walked over to him. "You look happy."

He set the box down then waved her away. "What else do you need me to do?"

"Well." She led him back to the hall closet and handed him another box. "You can start by cheering up. This goes in the kitchen."

Mike followed Michelle into the kitchen and set the box down. He could feel his face burning, whether from hurt or anger, he didn't know, or care. He wasn't used to it. In fact, it was something completely new, and it was completely related to his fight with Ricki, if that was what just happened between them. Except Ricki wasn't his girl, so how could what just happened be a fight? And if Ricki is my girl, he thought, the last thing we should be doing is fighting. He either wanted to hide under his bed or grab a bottle of something and settle in for the night. No glass. Just bottle and Mike, the two of them. Ease his sorrows. Except Michelle directed him to the silverware drawer.

"Empty that out." She pointed at the drawer. "Then vacuum out the crud and wipe it out with a damp cloth, then cut a piece of this—" she grabbed a roll of shelf paper "—to fit the bottom of the drawer."

She walked out of the kitchen, probably to resume the closet work. He bumbled around the drawer, fishing out the pieces of flatware, then realized he could just lift out the entire tray of utensils. It was women's work, not that he minded helping his sister, but this task required small hands and a nimble touch, not the stubby logs his fingers felt like. He tried lifting out the tray carefully from the drawer, but pulled out everything instead. The drawer dropped, the tray dropped, too, and knives and forks scattered everywhere. The crash brought Michelle into the kitchen.

"What's wrong with you?"

Mike's nerves were shot. He wanted to be anyplace but in the same room with his sister. Doing tedious chores was making him crazy.

"Nothing! I'm a klutz, okay?"

"It's that girl."

"Why don't you just leave for a while?"

"You trying to get rid me?"

"Maybe I wanna be alone. Maybe I don't feel like doing this shit."

He stood there, scraping at the kitchen wallpaper with his fingernail, too pissed to move. Michelle moved in, began to clean up the silverware, the tray, the drawer. She put the silverware in the dishwasher, replaced the drawer and put the tray in the sink. The whole time he just watched her do it. It took her all of three minutes. He felt like a jerk but did not try and stop her or even help. She slammed the drawer shut with her hip.

"So. Don't do this shit." She grabbed the roll of shelf paper and cut a sheet to fit the drawer.

"I'm sorry."

"Did you just now drop off Ricki?"

"Yeah." He stared out the window. The ash tree outside had fully leafed out. The color was fresh and new, the leaves a little translucent, brightly tinged in a yellow that would deepen into summer's rich green.

"You gonna see her again?"

He shook his head. "Hmm-mmm."

"Why not?"

"Look who she is. I don't want a girl like that. She colors her hair weird, runs around with man-hating females; she lies. She made up that whole post about me. It ruined my business."

Michelle tipped her head at him. Her face looked the certain way she did when she was seeing something besides the topic of conversation at hand and was about to call him out on it. He hated whenever she did it.

"You're wrong. Your business will survive, and that girl's a keeper."

"You're crazy. She's a freak, and I don't do freaks."

"When was the last time she looked that way?"

He thought—he'd seen her now twice since the night of the rally. Today, and at her parents' house yesterday. Neither of those times had she worn the black glop. And her hair was that pretty shade of blonde he liked so much. He wished she would grow it longer, except . . . no, he didn't wish. He didn't wish anything. How could he wish, when she'd given him every chance today to make her his girl, practically begged him; and he was such a jerk he almost kicked her out of his truck. Was it fear? He didn't know. He'd never put himself in this position with any girl before.

"The first time I met her."

"Right. She's changed since then. I've seen it. You've seen it. You just haven't paid attention. She's in love with you."

"That's crazy."

"You think so? You never bring girls here, but you brought her here after the rally so she could clean up. I saw it then. I saw the way you looked at her, and she liked it. You brought her here to get my approval, admit it. Well, you've got it."

He glared at her and plunged his hand into his pockets. "I don't need your approval."

"Say whatever you want. Did you even read her new blog post?"

"No."

"Oh, well, let me enlighten you." Michelle took his elbow and led him to the living room. She steered him to the armchair across from the couch. "Sit."

She grabbed some sheets of paper from the desk and stood in front of the fireplace as though she were addressing an audience. It was probably the printout of the post. He knew damn well why he hadn't read it. Just the name *Petra's Parlance* pissed him off all over again. Hurt, too, and he didn't want to feel that way anymore.

It was all just words. Except, her tears today on the phone when she asked him for help getting into her house—weren't just words. But tears didn't count. They, like words, were just another weapon wielded by females to manipulate guys like him.

She hadn't colored her hair. That wasn't words, either. And posting a blog, even though it was words, was a big risk she took. And now, Michelle was about to enlighten him, whether he wanted enlightenment or not. He tensed up, trying to brace himself for the emotional blows to come.

"*It was a lie from the start,*" read Michelle. "*All of it. I knew exactly what I was doing. I did it anyway. An act of complete cowardice. I betrayed a great movement, a great president, some very nice people, but most of all, a wonderful man. For readers of my previous post, I must renounce that.*

"*And so, this blog is a big mea culpa to all the great people at last week's rally, and to one man in particular. I hope he can find forgiveness in his heart, because I damaged him most of all . . .*

Michelle lowered the page and looked straight at him.

"Don't look at me that way," he said. His heart, his soul, were screaming in pain right now. Ricki had caused immense suffering and that suffering seemed to be playing through his whole being.

"Should I stop reading?"

"Yes, I can't take it."

"Too bad. I'm not done yet. But I'll skip down the page and read the pertinent part."

"*At one time in my life, I thought that destroying marriage would be a great step for society to take. And now the very thing I wanted to destroy, in the space of 48 hours, is something I very much want now for myself, my future . . .*"

Mike was still hurting, but he no longer hurt for himself. He hurt for Ricki. There would be her shock at seeing the truth of what she had done, and the pain of rejection of her friends over telling that new truth. She'd come through a lot, in a very short time. Her lies had hurt him; the fallout had disrupted his business, but the protests had subsided; in fact, her courageous act had drawn off the attack dogs, and they instead had focused on her. She had to have known what would happen, yet she'd been willing to live with the consequences. She'd done the right thing. He owed her his thanks, an apology. He owed her a truth of his own.

"I'm ready to accept the role of adult acting in the real world. I can't see how I ever had such a negative view of the world, and I now pity and loathe those people who do. It's wrong and they should stop. And I have to credit my newfound beliefs on a certain gentleman, with old-fashioned values, like our grandparents once had. There is virtue in those values, and I want them for myself . . . "

Michelle stopped. "There's more."

Mike put up his hand. "I've heard enough." He couldn't stand the feelings ripping through him right now. The words must be true. She'd have to have thought them, typed them, and pushed the publish button knowing the blowback to come, and she'd done it anyway. It took courage to do that. Courage and guts.

"She's talking to you, Mike. She's in love with you."

He doubted it. It was too risky for him to believe it was true. "She could be lying. She's done it before. Why should I believe it?"

"Because I saw it happen." Michelle pointed to the desk chair. "Right there. Today. We read the blog together. I asked her to show it to me, so she read it out loud. She changed while she was reading it. Her face, her voice, everything."

He narrowed his eyes. "What do you mean?"

"When she read the part to me that I just finished, she changed. I don't know, her voice got low, her face kind of screwed up, her bottom lip stuck out. I thought she might cry. She was very emotional. That was when she fell in love with you. I know women, don't doubt me."

Mike didn't know what to say. He couldn't speak anyway. There was a lump in his throat the size of an egg. His shell of anger was dissolving away. In its place was a sense of urgency, a need to right his own wrong, and fast, while he still had time.

"And what's more . . . " Michelle paused for so long he looked up to see if she was going to continue speaking.

He knew what was coming. "Don't say it," he said.

"I'm saying it," Michelle said. "And you're in love with her, too."

He hated the fact that she was right, and she'd said it out loud. He wondered if he'd be able to tell Ricki when he saw her again. If he'd ever even get the chance. When he looked back at Michelle, she was staring at him, her brows were raised, in question.

"You should probably go talk to her."

He rose, picked up his keys. "I guess so." He sat down again. "I'd better think this over a little bit. I need to work up my courage."

"Oh, I almost forgot," said Michelle.

"Now what?"

"She's getting a tattoo this afternoon."

He came out of his chair. He couldn't let her do that. "What? I don't like tattoos on women. Did she say when?"

Michelle shrugged. "I didn't ask. She didn't say."

"Well, did she tell you where?"

"Yeah, place called Covington—"

"That dump? I've got to talk her out of it. Did you tell her how I feel about them?"

"No. Why would I? I don't care if she gets five tattoos. In fact, it made me think of getting one myself."

"They're permanent. God only knows what it will look like." But wait. He sat down, then looked up at Michelle. "I can't tell her not to do it. I don't even have the right to ask her not to."

Michelle just glared at him. "Yeah. You don't have the right. But why do you even care? She's not your girl."

"I know," he said. "She's not my girl. But maybe . . . " He yanked on his ball cap and sprinted out the door before he finished his thought.

CHAPTER EIGHTEEN

In the space of two hours, Ricki had gone from dreading the pain of this procedure to welcoming it. The pain on her hip, she hoped, would blanket the pain in her heart—pain of a different sort caused by Mike's absence in her life.

She studied a printout of the design she'd chosen, and thought past the needles and instead focused on the resulting art—the capital letter R in elaborate, feminine script combined into the stem and leaves of a large, very red rose, Ricki's favorite flower.

The store was brightly lit, with white walls and a plush, elegant lobby with oriental carpets on the floor. The atmosphere mattered, for she preferred the look and feel of a luxury spa over gritty and urban. The day was warm. She'd worn a loose, tank-top style cotton dress, now pulled up to expose her right hip as she lay on an elevated bed. It would be a simple matter when finished to cover herself.

To pass the time while she waited for Jenna to begin, she watched the comings and goings on the sidewalk and street outside the windows. She was managing not to think of Mike, and then she saw him walk through the door. She blinked and waited for her breath to return, while she expected him to disappear, but he didn't. Instead, he looked around the place, maybe inspecting the construction work for quality. It seemed to meet with his approval. When he spotted her on the bed and their eyes met, she knew it wasn't just an image conjured up by wishes. The bed seemed to melt away. She felt suspended, for a moment, in midair.

He was motioning to her. The tattoo artist was fiddling with her supplies.

"Excuse me," Ricki said. "Can he come back here?"

Jenna looked at Mike, then shrugged and motioned to a nearby stool. "Up to you."

Ricki motioned him back. She pulled her dress down over her bared hip and sat up on the bed.

"Why are you here?" She whispered, loudly.

Mike answered her in his normal voice. "I was going to ask you the same thing."

"Because I want to do this."

"Why, because everybody has one?"

"I like them. I've always wanted one." She wanted him to understand, although why she cared was something she could not fathom. Except, the sight of him walking through the door changed everything. The tattoo's importance fell away; it was replaced with new hope. She'd come from wondering how she could forget him, to his physical presence right here, next to her. His approval, or disapproval, mattered now.

She lowered her voice. "It's important, Mike. To me."

"What if I don't want you to do it?"

"Why do you care? Two hours ago, you wouldn't even look at me. Now, you want to run my life?"

"No, I don't want to run your life. I just want you to think about what you're about to do."

"I have thought about it. Since I was eight and couldn't get one for my birthday."

"Yeah, but that was before me."

"Not that it matters, but what do you have against tattoos?"

"Women shouldn't have tattoos. I don't like them at all, especially not on women."

"Nobody thinks that way anymore."

"Except me. Ricki, you're looking at a guy who lives his grandfather's values."

"Sure," she said it a bit wearily. "How could I forget, ladies first. You have no right to say anything about this."

From her supply cabinet, Jenna was watching them. "There's chairs in the lobby if you want to discuss this. You'll be more comfortable."

They went out and sat on a cushioned bench. Mike reached out and softly stroked her bare shoulder. "Ricki," he said, "look at me."

She raised her eyes to his. His look was as soft as his touch. "It's permanent," he said. "It scars. It's disrespectful to the perfect body that God gave you."

It was a point that Ricki could not answer. She'd thought a lot about tattoos during her life, but never as disfiguring, always as adornment. But ever since she knew Mike, he'd given her new things to think about, new ways to see the world.

He took her hand in his and studied their intertwined fingers. "I'm an old-fashioned guy, but even I know enough that I can't forbid you to do this. So I'm going to ask you. Don't do this, just yet. Not for me, but for us."

"Us, what do you mean us?"

"Michelle read me your *mea culpa* blog post."

"Oh?" Ricki was feeling dizzy from this. It was the last thing she expected to happen, after he rejected her in the truck.

"I didn't realize . . . you wrote 'I want those values for myself.'"

She nodded slowly. "Your grandfather's values—your values. But if I couldn't have you, I still want your values. They're my values, too, now."

"If you could have me, would you still want me?"

"Of course, I would. Why would I settle for second best if I can have you?"

"I love you, Ricki. I fell in love with you when I first helped you through the trolley car door that day—green hair, black lipstick, and all. I kept watch over you that day."

He lowered his voice. "It was brave and spunky for you to attend the rally, to go over to the other side. But there was danger, too. I had to make sure you got out of there safely. And I wanted a chance to talk to you."

Ricki leaned in, close. She couldn't believe this was happening. "I want you to forgive me for what I did," she said. "That's why I wrote the second post. Even if you wouldn't see me again, at least know that I was sorry . . . am sorry."

"It's okay, Ricki, all of it. All this bad stuff will go away—the business protest will pass; the mobs, your blog posts—they'll be forgotten in days, if not sooner. After that, there's us—just us. But this ink—it's just plain ugly."

Jenna appeared from the back room. "Ricki, if you want to do this, we need to get started. I have another session booked in two hours."

Ricki looked at Mike. "Well?"

He shrugged. "If it means not having you, then get the tattoo, but maybe we could talk about it first?"

"Okay, I'll wait. But you have to promise me we will talk about it."

"Of course, I promise. My grandfather wouldn't let me forget it."

Ricki turned to Jenna and tucked her hand possessively into Mike's arm. "I've decided to wait."

Mike spoke up. "Sorry for the inconvenience. How much for your trouble today?"

Jenna checked her book at the desk. "For today, $150."

Mike took out his wallet and dropped a hundred and a fifty on the counter. He swept Ricki up into a kiss. She stepped away, breathless. "I think I'm hungry."

Mike laughed. "Hungry? We'd better get you something to eat."

Arm in arm, they walked out the door of the tattoo parlor. Mike took his phone from his pocket.

"Who are you calling?" said Ricki

"The diner," said Mike. "To see if they take reservations. My girl's hungry and I don't want her to wait."

THE END

AUTHOR BIO

Liberty Adams lives in the wide, open spaces west of the Rockies. She writes wholesome, lighthearted romance about patriots who love America, love our president, and, best of all, fall in love at the end of each story. Liberty is the pen name of an author who wears the hats of mom, wife, and community volunteer. She proudly owns and wears several assorted MAGA hats of her own.

A NOTE TO READERS

The readers of these stories are the best of America. You live your values every day through faith, hard work, and raising and protecting your families. You have your own unique stories to tell about how you came to support this President. The MAGA Hat Romance series was written with you in mind.

If you enjoyed reading "Ladies First," by Liberty Adams, please leave a review on Amazon. It's a great way to spread the MAGA word!

Here is a preview of my new story, Book II in the MAGA Hat Romance series, "Almost a Family."

Four years ago, Allie was left widowed with a newborn infant to raise. For the sake of their daughter, Allie honors her husband's memory by being supermom and rejecting all relationships and dating. But on a family cruise, Allie finds herself in the presence of the handsome, eligible ship's doctor more than she would like.

Dr. Matt Wilson took the cruise ship job after a broken engagement. He can't help but fall in love with Allie, even though he sees her at her worst moments. Sensing Allie's protectiveness toward her daughter, he makes her an offer impossible to resist. Can Allie break with her past and accept a new daddy for her daughter, and let herself love again?

For more of the MAGA Hat Romance series,
visit **magahatromance.com**.

Check out Book III, Justice for Mary Beth, the latest in the MAGA Hat Romance series:

Mary Beth Halloran, real estate developer and Trump volunteer, is on the verge of making her dreams come true: a meeting with President Trump and, crossed fingers, a career with the Trump organization. The meeting and the job are hers if she can just snag the last voter on her list and get him to answer four little questions.

Alone in his mountain lair, Justice K. Journey has no patience for the trespassing female who pesters him about his land and his politics. He won't answer her questions and, most of all, Journey Hollow isn't for sale. His great-grandaddy, Justice, swung from a rope trying to defend the Journey land from interlopers. Justice won't give up his heritage, or the rights to the water that gushes from the spring above his house.